The Ninja Librarian

Rebecca M. Douglass

This is a work of fiction. Names, characters, places, and incidents are products of the author's imagination and are not to be construed as real. Any resemblance to actual events, locales, organizations, or persons, living or dead, is entirely coincidental.

DEDICATION

To Laurie, who kept asking for more stories until I found myself with a book, and has given valuable input every step of the way. And, of course, to Tom, the original Ninja Librarian, who gave me the idea in the first place.

CONTENTS

ACKNOWLEDGMENTS

Many thanks to Lisa Frieden, whose editing saved me from many errors (those which remain are purely my responsibility). Thanks also go always to my husband Dave, who has supported me in every way through all my writing. Special appreciation goes to Danielle English for the cover art, to Steve Tse for cover design, and to Walter Merchant for the interior illustrations.

THE NINJA LIBRARIAN

S kunk Corners is hard on librarians. Murderously hard on them, if you believe what Wild Harry Colson and Crazy Jake say. Even if they're stretching the truth a mite, it's true we haven't had a librarian stick it out here for more than a few weeks since the tough element took over some while back.

So when Tom—that was all the name he gave when he got off the train and saw us all staring— came to take over the Skunk Corners library, betting in town ran about fifty to one against him lasting two days. Hadn't the last librarian been more'n six feet tall, weighed 200 pounds, and still only made it ten days? This Tom character was not so tall, not so big, and edging on towards old. His only really impressive feature was his full head of white hair.

There was something about that hair, and the intensely blue eyes that met mine when I got closer, that struck me. That's why I matched those fifty bets. Everyone in town thought I was a chump for taking the bets, though no one said so, because no one here is dumb enough to call Big Al a fool. Of course, Tom only had to last forty-nine hours for me to collect on the bets, but once the bets were made, there were fifty men, women, and children in town bent on making sure they collected, so he faced more than the usual hostility. Since I didn't have the cash to pay up, I was equally bent on making him stay.

Tom hit Skunk Corners on the afternoon train, and disappeared straightaway into the library, the only brick building on Main Street. Which, Main being pretty much the only street in the Corners, made it the only brick building in town, period.

The library and the school occupied the far end of the street from the depot, so to get there he had to walk right past pretty much everyone in town. He glanced at the Mercantile, raised an eyebrow at the tavern and the bank sitting cheek-by-jowl, and nodded just a bit as he took in the imposing false front of our City Hall, which forms one side of our town square, a big name for a little patch of dirt. Then the librarian unlocked the door of the library and disappeared inside.

I watched him go, and then went back to work. But I made a point of sticking around the schoolhouse, casual-like, when the young 'uns got out, and eavesdropped on them bragging and boasting about how they'd run the new bookworm off. Funny, how they take against librarians, but mostly let their teacher alone. Not that they put much effort into their schooling, mind, but they don't run

Teacher off, either. At least, no one's tried since I came to town.

When the kids had all scattered, I wandered down to Two-Timin' Tess's tavern for a while and listened to the guys making their boasts about how they'd clobber the fellow and dump him on the noon train. I had to give the youngsters credit for having more imagination than their elders. Finally I headed on down to Johnson's Mercantile, where the women were making their plans. Skunk Corners had it in for librarians, no question, and this Tom character had his work cut out for him, and that was just for surviving, let alone running a library.

I prowled around until dark, picking up a hint here and a notion there. Mostly folks seemed to figure on making a move when the library opened in the morning, so it occurred to me that if Tom just didn't open up, he'd be okay. It was with the intention of suggesting that he just lie low a while that I snuck in at the back door of the library.

I didn't knock, of course, just slipped my knife blade in at the bolt and popped it open, the way I've always done when I want a book. I couldn't go in the front door and let the whole town see Big Al checking out a book like just anyone. Not that much of anyone did check books out. A few took what they wanted, and brought them back if they felt like it, but most just went in to gawp at all the books they wouldn't know how to read, even if they wanted to. And they went in to make life miserable for the librarians, of course.

I stepped into the dark building—Tom hadn't seemed to feel the need for a light, or maybe he was too scared to show one—and stopped short. There he was, right in front of me. I mean, I never saw or heard him coming; he was just *there*.

For one moment, I felt a little scared, but then I had to laugh at myself. Me, Big Al, scared of little white-

haired Tom-the-Librarian? It was just the surprise of
seeing him there. If any of the previous librarians
ever knew I'd snuck in, they'd hidden somewhere far
from my path, because I never saw them. This one
just stood still in front of me, moonlight through the
windows lighting up the black silk handkerchief
folded just so in his breast pocket.

"May I help you?"

Crazy as it sounds, that mild inquiry convinced me
I'd made the right bet. I mean, if he was so eager to
please, surely he'd listen to reason and just hole up
here for a while. Maybe I could convince him the
town's grudge would wear off if they didn't see him
for two or three days. Just long enough for me to win
my bet.

I laid it all out for him, not the bets, but the plans.
The primer kids' plans to bring in a skunk. The
ladies' ipecac casseroles. And the toughs at the tavern
who'd most likely just pick a fight and flatten him.
He listened in silence. Then he said, still in that polite,
mild voice,

"Thank you. I do not anticipate any problems."

I goggled at him. Gaped. Stared, with my jaw
down around my knees.

"Didn't you hear any a' what I was sayin', Mister?
If the kids and the ladies don' worry you—but they
oughta—you gotta know Wild Harry Colson and
Crazy Jake and them will just chew you up and spit
you out." I know how to talk almost like an educated
soul, but he surprised me right into talking like a
local.

Then he said the strangest thing, the thing I
thought was a joke, or bravado, or just plain lunacy.
He said,

"You need not worry about my safety. I am
trained to kill."

About then, I decided to hightail it out of there. Craziness might be catching, and I didn't want any of that.

Well, I cleared out, and next morning the library opened at Ten O'clock sharp, just the way the sign out front had always said, though mostly it didn't. Open, I mean. Because there usually wasn't a librarian, or he'd be in the back, packing to leave town. Sometimes he'd be hiding under the bed.

I came in the usual way and kept watch through the wide crack in the door leading back into the librarian's quarters. I didn't figure it would do me any good to be seen around there, and someone might get it into his head that there was more than one way to get out of paying off that bet with me. So I kept out of sight and watched.

Not much happened at first. A few youngsters filtered in, ones I recognized as trouble. Then a couple of the ladies came with their covered dishes, all warm and friendly and welcoming. I knew better, of course. If Tom ate that stuff, he'd spend the rest of the day in the outhouse out back, at least until the big kids came and tipped it over on him.

Tom greeted the boys and pointed them to the children's books, a half dozen or so ragged volumes in one corner. I could have told him they couldn't read.

I should know, being their teacher, but I wasn't giving up my hiding place to share that old news.

When the ladies came, Tom accepted the hot dishes with thanks and put them on the windowsill, to be ready for lunch, he said. Then he sat down at the desk and began trying to make sense of the lender cards he'd found in some drawer or other. They must have made for bewildering reading, because I know for a fact no one has filled out a card in years. Not since Skunk Corners decided they had no use for librarians, nor for libraries, either, and that was back before my time.

Things stayed pretty quiet for the first hour or so. The kids in the corner did a lot of snickering, and I figured they were rigging some kind of booby-trap, or maybe just waiting for their cohorts to arrive with the town's namesake animal. The ladies wandered off, some picking up a book or two on their way, but making no move to sign them out. Tom just watched, and didn't try to interfere, and I figured he'd seen the way things were, after all.

Just before noon, Crazy Jake and Wild Harry Colson came in, and I braced myself for the inevitable. Nothing happened right off. They had to wait to catch Tom's attention, and he didn't seem to be terribly interested in them.

When a half dozen more boys came in carrying a box, Harry seemed to take it as a signal. Maybe he figured he'd better get on with it before the skunk cut loose. He let fly with a gob of tobacco spit onto the floor just in front of where Tom had stepped over to examine a bookshelf. Tom looked up and said, as though to a not-too-bright child,

"The spittoon is in the corner. Please make use of it in the future, sir."

Harry and Jake took the cue. They spat on the floor again and swaggered up to the diminutive librarian.

"Wha'd you say, bookworm?"

"I requested that you expectorate in the appropriate receptacle," came the incomprehensible response. The two toughs exchanged bewildered glances, before deciding how to take that.

"Ain't nobody talks to me that way," Harry snarled, and went into action.

The boys in the corner took his move as their signal, too, opening the box to release the dazed and unhappy black-and-white animal they'd somehow managed to trap without getting sprayed. Wild Harry Colson and Crazy Jake took another step toward the cornered librarian, and I looked away from the crack in the door, just for a moment. I couldn't help it. I hated to see the man go down. He'd made a brave stand, after all.

I jammed my eye back to that crack in time to see Tom, a black mask across his face, drop Harry and Jake with a pair of matched blows to the back of the head—opposite sides, one with each hand—then whirl and smack the skunk, just in the process of raising its tail, with a neat kick under its middle. He booted it gently out the door.

It was too bad for the townsfolk, crowded around the entrance to see the fun, that the skunk got all systems together and started spraying just as it cleared the doorway. I don't think it missed a one of them, and Johnson's Mercantile sold out of tinned tomato juice after the first five customers.

I pulled my attention back to the interior, and watched Tom catch Wild Harry Colson as he fell, somehow keeping him in motion to pitch him straight out the window, sweeping it clear of hot dishes on his way through. Crazy Jake went down like a ton of bricks; even the Ninja Librarian, as I now knew him to be, wasn't fast enough to catch both those former toughs on the way down. He never looked my way, but addressed the air.

"Come on out and lend a hand with this debris, Alice." Maybe it was the surprise of him knowing my real name, when some folks in town still didn't even know I was a girl, but I did as I was told.

When we'd deposited Jake at the bottom of the steps, the librarian brushed his hands off on his trousers, pulled the mask off and tucked it neatly into his breast pocket, where it once again resembled the black silk handkerchief I'd taken it for last night. Reentering the library, we looked around the now-empty room.

Tom cleared his throat with a deprecating "ahem," and finally looked at me as he spoke.

"Does that completely answer your question?"

I had no idea what he meant, but I learned.

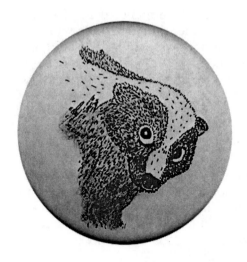

THE NINJA LIBRARIAN VS. THE STORY TIME TODDLERS

I slunk into the Skunk Corners library one afternoon to find Tom, our librarian, looking glum. I come in the front door these days, during business hours. Tom convinced me to do that, but he can't make me comfortable doing it.

"Alice," he'd said—Tom's the only one in Skunk Corners calls me Alice. Mostly I'm Big Al, or just Al. I never did figure out how he knew my name, but he'd pegged me right off and wouldn't let me forget it. "Alice, you might just as well come in the front door. No more sneaking in the back after dark."

"But—" I protested.

"You're the teacher, Alice."

"I never set out to be," I muttered.

"That is not germane to the issue. You are the teacher, and therefore everyone knows you can read. So you might as well admit it. Flaunt it, even."

I wasn't convinced, but Tom's not just any librarian. He's the Ninja Librarian, and I didn't feel like arguing. So I came in the front door that day, like I said, and there was Tom, settin' at his desk looking like his dog just died.

Seems he was discouraged that no one much came into the library.

"Well," I said. "You threw out the bad element." So he had. They'd landed on most of the rest of the townsfolk, along with an agitated skunk.

"The problem," he said with a sad smile, "is that throwing them out seems to have discouraged the entire populace."

It was true. People around here are a little scared of Tom, to be honest. They don't like things they can't understand, which was the main problem they had with libraries in the first place. Before Tom came, we hadn't managed to keep a librarian above a week since Adam ate the apple.

I offered what consolation I could. "Things stay nice and tidy in here now."

He shook his head. "That won't do. Tidiness at a library isn't a good sign, Alice. If I can't improve circulation, or at least attendance, the library will be shut down."

That got my attention. "They wouldn't!" Though come to think of it, I didn't know who "they" were.

"They would."

"Well." I thought of a new tack. "What do other libraries do?"

He thought a moment, then brightened right up. "Story time!"

"Story time?"

"Of course. For the children too young for your school."

I shook my head. "I don't know. I'm not sure you want that sort in here." He didn't take my meaning, either through ignorance or deliberate intent.

"Of course we want the little children," he beamed. "Start them early, and they'll be readers all their lives." And keep coming to the library, I could see he was thinking.

"I dunno," I began.

"I sense you are dubious," Tom said. "I assure you it's what all the libraries do. In any case, I believe I can handle anyone in Skunk Corners."

"Yes," I admitted. "But they're babies. You can't throw them out the door if they misbehave."

His face fell as he realized the truth of what I said. But then he squared his shoulders. "Perhaps not. But if so many libraries do it, surely we can manage as well."

We? I didn't like the sound of that.

"Me, I've got a school to teach. You're on your own, mister." What's more, I couldn't help thinking that those other libraries weren't in Skunk Corners, but I couldn't bring myself to discourage him further by saying so.

Next day, a notice appeared on the library door: "Story time for all children up to school age, Thursday, 11:00 a.m."

One thing I knew, I'd have to be there to watch what happened on Thursday, though I'd surely not be out front where I could get drawn into the disaster.

I sent my students out to recess Thursday at eleven and snuck off to the library. I popped open the back door, the way I hadn't done for several weeks, and snuck up the hall. Eleven was several minutes gone by the time I pressed my eye to the crack in the door—the one I'd enlarged with my belt knife so I could spy without straining my eyes.

Story time was just getting started. Tom stood by his desk, his hands moving vaguely, as though trying to contain the chaos before him.

Always interested in any change from their stultifying routines, all the young mothers had come. The floor was covered with critters of the creeping, crawling, and toddling kind. That wasn't so bad; I figured it was the three- and four-year-olds climbing the shelves that made Tom look so sick. None of the mothers seemed to consider any of this out of line.

Finally he gave up trying to get the children, or their mothers, to quiet down, and just sat down and started in to reading, which seemed as good a plan as any.

The story was "The Three Little Pigs," and half a dozen toddlers began crying because they thought a wolf would come eat them. Buddy Clooney bucked the trend. He cried because the wolf got killed and didn't get to eat any of the pigs. Buddy's four, and I don't think he gets enough to eat, most days.

The few children not crying by the end of the first story started in to howl when he pulled out the next, "Goldilocks and the Three Bears." A few eventually stopped, but only because they had found books to chew on, going to town on them with their sharp little baby teeth.

I couldn't watch any longer. I crept back to the school, sure that Tom would give up the crazy idea and content himself with checking books out to me and the half-dozen other literate residents of Skunk Corners.

But when I dropped by after school I found Tom full of plans for the next time.

"How did it go today?" I asked, pretending I hadn't been watching.

"Not so very badly," he answered, either lying through his teeth or dangerously deluded. I looked around and saw an immense pile of books waiting to be put back on the shelves. I lent a hand while Tom told me his plans.

"It is a bit of a challenge," he conceded. "I don't suppose the children are much accustomed to being read to."

I didn't suppose many had parents who could read if they wanted to, and fewer still who wanted to, but I kept my trap shut.

"Still, all I need to do is get them to sit still long enough to get interested in the stories."

"All!" Seemed like a tall order to me.

"I think I am capable, Alice," he said with dignity, and tapped the black silk in his breast pocket. I wondered what good his Ninja mask would do him this time.

The following Thursday I aligned my eye with the door-crack in the full expectation of a repeat of the previous week's disaster. Worse, in fact, as I'd seen most of the mothers outside, sharing some beverage in a canning jar and leaving their babies to Tom.

To my surprise, neat rows of toddlers sat quietly, listening while the white-haired librarian read a series of stories about puppies, butterflies, and fairies. A few shifted restlessly from time to time, and several drooled, but none made noise, and none moved from their positions in line.

I walked back to the school, mystified. It appeared that the Ninja Librarian had triumphed again, but how? His mask was still folded in his pocket. Did it contain special powers even beyond what I'd already seen?

I posed the question when I came to return my library book after school. Tom gave me a sly grin and held out a package of "Dottie's Best Giant Jawbreakers."

"Get one of these in their mouths and there's no room for noise."

"But how'd you get them to sit still?" I persisted. "I'd have thought they'd be crawling all over drooling sticky goo on the books."

"I'm the Ninja Librarian," Tom said, his blue eyes unreadable. "What I throw out stays out, and what I set in place stays where I put it." Not a word more would he utter on the topic. Nor did he offer his usual, "does that completely answer your question?" so I knew he was holding back. But nothing more could I get from him, try as I might.

Only as I was leaving did I notice the empty packages in the trash. I gave a small smile as I continued down the steps. Story time had come to Skunk Corners to stay. At least, for as long as the supply of flypaper held out.

Once again, I had completely answered my questions at my library.

THE NINJA LIBRARIAN AND THE SCHOLARS OF SKUNK CORNERS SCHOOL

W hat on earth was the Skunk Corners librarian doing with a face longer than a wet winter? His toddler story time had caught on, and the crowd every Thursday morning was large and surprisingly well-behaved. But here he was, moping and worried. Even his hair looked discouraged, and his blue eyes had gone grey.

I'd brought back my library book and was hunting for a new one. The Skunk Corners library has a nice brick building on Main Street, but the selection of books inside is limited. That's mostly because of all those years without a librarian, or at least without one who dared come out from under his bed. Until Tom came to town, the local toughs, led by Wild Harry Colson and Crazy Jake, had driven off every librarian and taken all the books they wanted. Luckily, they had little use for books, being mostly illiterate, so we still had some left.

But there'd been no one to send for new books for a long time, and I'd read most of the good stuff. I was set to ask Tom about getting more books when I noticed his long face.

"What's the trouble?" I asked, as kindly as I could. If I concentrate, I can be pleasant enough. "Story time is going well, isn't it? Or did you run out of fly paper?" It was the first time I'd revealed I knew how he kept the kiddies in line, and Tom gave me a sharp look. I met it with the same stony face that wins the big pots in the poker games at Two-Timin' Tess's Tavern, and he chose not to comment.

"The children are coming in, Alice. They even listen to the stories." He sighed. "But very few of them, or their mothers, check out books."

I nodded. "Can't read. And those that can, won't." Kind of like my students in the Skunk Corners School. I had my own problems, though I didn't care to bring them up when Tom seemed so low.

I'd been teaching the Skunk Corners School for over two years, ever since the previous teacher took off for greener pastures, back when I was sixteen. I don't know just where he lit, but I could bet it was an improvement on Skunk Corners.

Anyway, when Teacher Bentley left, folks looked around for a replacement. There was some talk of skipping the whole thing and closing the school, but Preacher Dawson said the state said we had to have schooling for the little ones. Someone else—I don't know who or I'd have pounded him—let on as how

Big Al could read and figure. Next thing I knew, I was the teacher. I was already "Big Al" then, but I lacked confidence, so I let them get away with it.

No one really expected me to do much, but the trouble was, now that I was teacher, I couldn't just let it go. Hardly a one of my students could read for beans, and it wasn't because I didn't try. I tried, but they wouldn't. I could make them sit still and I could make them shut up, but I couldn't make them listen, and I couldn't make them learn.

And I was fed up with it.

Tom watched me while I thought. Then he spoke up.

"Now, what seems to be bothering you, Alice?" Tom is the only person in town who doesn't call me Big Al. He's hard to intimidate, seeing as how he's not just any librarian. He's the Ninja Librarian, trained to kill, and with an answer for every question.

Every question? Was it possible he could solve my problem? That's when it hit me. If he could solve my problem, I could solve his.

"Well, now," I began. "I'm thinking my trouble is behind your trouble. See, my students can't read. Can't, or won't, learn—seems about fifty-fifty to me."

"Nonsense," Tom said. All signs of depression had vanished like a fresh bottle at Tess's. "Anyone can learn to read."

"Then I reckon they just won't." That discouraged me even worse, on account of it was me couldn't make them. But Tom looked happy as could be.

"Precisely. And a child who won't learn is a child who just hasn't met the right incentive."

The incentive, I could see, would come from our very own Ninja Librarian. I could feel my face trying to smile. And yet—

"How?" I mean, licking the tar out of them wouldn't help. I'd tried that.

Tom just tapped the side of his head. "You have to be smarter than them."

Well, that shouldn't be so hard. I was hurt by the implication that I wasn't smarter than those blockheads in my school.

Nothing more could I get out of Tom. He just declared he would come to the school for an hour every morning, and I would ready the library for opening while he dealt with my students.

I'd helped him out enough to know what to do, but I didn't completely like the arrangement. I wanted to see how he handled the problem. I mean, you can't make a kid learn to read by pitching him out the window headfirst. Can you? But I agreed to the terms, planning a sneak visit to the school to watch how he did it.

If he could do it.

We started the new program Monday morning. I let the kids into the schoolhouse, took roll, and then announced that we had a new reading teacher. I didn't tell them how confident he was about teaching them to read, since they might take that as a challenge and try to prove they couldn't learn. I just made the announcement and went to the door to let in Tom, who stood on the step with a small valise in his hand.

"I'll be back in an hour," I said, and walked on out past him, pocketing the library key which he had for some reason felt obliged to give me. As if I needed a key. As I walked away, I heard Tom's deceptively quiet voice saying,

"Now, children, you need to know two things. You all *can* learn to read. And you all *will* learn to read."

I wanted to keep listening, but I had to get the library ready. I hurried through the morning chores, but things were such an unexpected mess there that I didn't make it back more than a few minutes before ten, just in time to hear Tom concluding, "you've all done well, but it's just a start. I'll see you tomorrow." Then he walked out, carrying his valise, and I walked in.

None of the kids would tell me what he had done. "We promised we wouldn't say a word," Tommy Colson told me, his face innocent. I couldn't tell what he was feeling. Tommy is kin to Wild Harry Colson, and I wouldn't have expected him to keep a secret for a second, but when I pressed him, he cut his eyes from classmate to classmate, shrugged, and refused to say another word.

Matters went on like that for a couple of weeks. Tom showed up every day with his valise, but I never could get a glimpse of what might be in it. I noticed that the students were starting to act like they could read a bit when we did other lessons, though they tried to hide it. If they were going to read for Tom, and still refused to do so for me, I figured I'd have to leave town. To my surprise, the thought made me unhappy.

After two weeks, I had to know. I crept into the library late Sunday night, very, very quietly so that Tom wouldn't hear me, and did most of the set-up so I'd be free the next morning. Monday morning it took me only a few minutes to finish, and I snuck back to the schoolhouse. I'm just tall enough to see in the window while standing on the ground, and I chose the north side, where the shadows would keep anyone from noticing me. Nothing about the schoolhouse is soundproof—or weather-tight—so I could hear everything that went on.

Tom wanted to keep his approach a secret for some reason, but I was the teacher, darn it. I needed to know, or I'd be forever dependent on him to teach my kids to read. So I crept up to the window at a quarter past and peered over the sill. What I saw almost made me gasp, and I ducked back out of sight in a hurry as Tom's glance shifted toward me. It's hard to sneak up on a Ninja.

Inch by inch I raised myself until my eyes just topped the windowsill again. Across the top of the chalkboard Tom had printed, "You know you can read this," and below, "It's no use pretending. Begin working now."

All the children sat quietly at their desks, heads bent over their primers, some lips moving, some not, but every one of them studying his or her book for dear life. Occasionally someone would scribble a note on his slate, or raise her hand and Tom would come bend over and whisper something.

Each child had a toy or treasure of some sort sitting on his desk. Tommy Colson had a tin of chaw. I realized I hadn't seen those things around lately, and wondered why not. From time to time a child would reach out and touch his or her treasure, as though testing to be sure it was really there. Then they'd go back to reading.

That was it. They read for the better part of an hour, then Tom dismissed them to recess and I came around to the front door.

I tested the kids later, writing on the board, "Whatever I say, don't move or I'll toss you out the door." Then I tried saying all sorts of things, from "Recess!" to "Fire," to "free ice cream feed at the Methodist Church" (we have one—a church, I mean— and nearly everyone goes. They just don't seem to take in the message very well). Not a child stirred. Finally I gave a huge sigh.

"Okay, class. The jig's up. You've learned to read, and I'll not let you forget it."

I sought Tom out after school. He sat in his library, surrounded by books, and looked at me over the glasses he'd lately taken to wearing. I noticed he only wore them sometimes, mostly, I think, when he didn't want me to see his eyes too clearly.

I sat down on the only other chair in the library. No one else was there, so I asked straight out, "how'd you do it?"

"Alice, Alice," Tom chided. "You were watching. And you still have to ask?"

I scowled, an expression that sent most folks scurrying for cover. Tom didn't even flinch. "All I saw was you teaching them same as I've always done. I can't see any reason they learned for you and not for me."

He looked me in the eye. "That's right."

"Huh?"

"They learned for me exactly as well as they did for you."

"Huh?" I didn't get it. I mean, they couldn't read before, and they now they could. Of course something had changed.

"They could read when I went in there. Most of them could, at least. They just didn't want to let on."

"I'll be damned."

"Does that completely answer your question?" Tom asked, his face inscrutable.

"Goldurn it, Tom! No, it doesn't! How did you convince them to admit it?"

"You saw the message on the board." He wasn't asking.

"Yeah."

"The first day, I wrote, 'you are a bunch of idiots who will never learn to read this.' About five kids blurted out that they were not and they'd punch me out if I said it again. That's when I changed it to the message you saw. After that, it was a matter of practice."

"Huh." I was sure there was more to it than that, but I could see I wasn't going to get anything more out of him. Anyway, I had a hunch. I was thinking about the valise and those treasures on the desks— they were out of sight by the time I came into the classroom, but I'd seen them. Things I hadn't seen for weeks, not since Tom had started teaching.

By the gods! He'd taken hostages, carted their treasures off in his valise and not given them back until they would read. I smiled, and Tom saw it, but we didn't need to say anything.

"And now," Tom said, "What are you going to do about my problem?"

It took me a moment to remember Tom's problem. There weren't enough books being checked in and out. But the solution popped into my head right off, and I smiled.

"Library day, of course. Every child, all twenty-three, checks out one book every week. You'd better start ordering more books for the kids. And, while you're at it, could you get a few more for me?" I met his look, and took a deep breath. Then I let him have it. The line he used on me every time I asked him anything:

"Does that completely answer your question?"

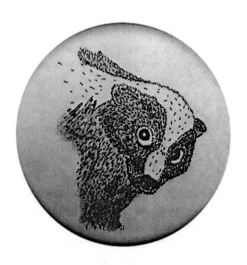

THE NINJA LIBRARIAN AND THE WIDOWS

T hings were awfully quiet in Skunk Corners. My students, having discovered they could read, were mostly working hard on their lessons. Tommy Colson had a tendency to sit at his desk, chewing tobacco and staring into space as though trying to comprehend something unfathomable. I didn't push it. I figured geography might well be unfathomable to someone who'd never been beyond Skunk Corners, and math tough for someone with no more than one of anything.

Down at the library, the Ninja Librarian hadn't needed to pitch anyone out for over a week. When Tom throws you out of the library, you know you've been ejected, and most folks don't need to repeat the lesson. He's a mild-looking, white-haired gentleman with the calm voice and quiet manner befitting a librarian. But that's no black silk hanky in his breast pocket. It's a Ninja mask, and transforms him in an instant to a lethal fighting machine.

Not that he's killed anyone in Skunk Corners.

Yet.

Like I say, things were pretty quiet when I began noticing an increase in business at the library. In particular, a lot of the Skunk Corners widows had developed a sudden hankering for books. And an amazing lot of them just happened to have some extra cake, cookies, or casserole to bring along for "the poor dear," and unlike the casseroles some of the ladies brought when Tom first arrived, these didn't have any nasty additions. It didn't take a genius to see what was up, but Tom just accepted the offerings as though there was nothing unusual about it—and passed them off to me for my students.

The scholars at the Skunk Corners School liked the cookies and cakes best, but there were those who surely needed the hot dishes, because they never did get enough to eat. Tommy Colson was one of my hungriest. Tom had gotten him to read, and to admit he could, but it was those widows who were solving his other problem, the one that made him sullen and angry: hunger.

I wandered over to the library like I did most days after school let out, just to enjoy the quiet and maybe chat a bit with Tom.

To my dismay, the usually quiet library was a buzz of shrill voices and a blur of gray hair. Like I say, the hot-dish brigade had been going for a while, but this was something else. I stopped dead in the doorway and tried to count. They were moving around a lot, jockeying for a spot near the librarian's desk, so it wasn't easy, but I'm pretty sure there were at least a dozen women in there, every one of them widowed and looking.

There were even two or three ladies I didn't recognize, and that could only mean one thing: word had spread. They must've come in from nearby towns, maybe from Two-Bit to the north, or Lupine to the south. That latter was named for a right pretty flower, but it was a God-forsaken spot, and any right-thinking woman would be happy to leave, even to come to Skunk Corners.

I couldn't really blame the ladies, and their food was helping my students, but I knew one thing: if this kept up, the ladies would succeed in doing what had stumped all the rowdies and toughs in town. They'd drive the Ninja Librarian out of here, back to wherever he came from.

The crowd was starting to get to Tom. He maintained his outward calm, but I spotted the way his eyes darted from side to side, as though seeking an escape route. There was only one thing to do, and I did it. I would rather have cut and run, because aside from catching Tom, these ladies wanted nothing so much as to reform me, but I marched right into that room.

"Tom, I need you to go down and hunt up something in the paper for me." The Skunk Corners Library had a collection of newspapers in the basement, dating from away back when the town had a paper for a year or two. That was before the editor had been run out of town for printing too much truth.

Tom looked at me, surprise and relief visible for a fraction of a second before his inscrutable calm returned.

"What do you require, Alice?" His cultured voice revealed nothing.

"I'll write it down for you," I offered, pulling a scrap of paper and stub of pencil from a pocket.

I tell you, pockets are the number one reason I dress like a fellow. Ladies' clothes never have enough places to stow stuff. They're meant to carry big bags around for all their needfuls, but me, I like to keep my hands free. It's safer when things get rough.

I scrawled, "get out while you can," on the paper and said aloud, "I'll watch the shop while you look. I imagine it'll take a while."

Tom understood, and he grabbed his chance with both hands. "Why, thank you, Alice. Feel free to use my desk and mark your papers while you keep an eye on things." Then he disappeared through the rear door and I was left alone with the little old ladies.

A silence fell over the room as I went to sit at Tom's desk. I laid down a pile of essays my students had turned in that day, opened a drawer to find a pen, and glared at the crowd.

"Line to check out books forms to my left," I informed them. "Leave the food on the back table, and pick up your empties." Most of the women left their offerings, and rooted through the dishes the students and I had washed and returned, before leaving. A few of the more savvy ladies lined up to check out books, thereby giving themselves an excuse to come back. The out-of-town ladies looked daggers at me. They couldn't take books, and they needed to work fast. It's not that easy to get up here from much of anywhere, even Two-Bit, which is the nearest town to Skunk Corners. So they couldn't count on coming back real soon.

Within a quarter hour the crowd had dispersed, and I'd made a start at marking the papers. After a half hour, Tom peeped around the door, saw the empty room, and came in. He pulled up a chair from the reading table, and took some of the essays to look over.

"Thank you, Alice. I confess I did not know just what to do." A wry smile twisted his lips. "A Ninja's training does not extend to the treatment of amorous widows."

"You're welcome." I tried to maintain a dignified tone, but could feel a grin spreading over my face. Big Al had managed something the Ninja Librarian couldn't.

My smile faded. I couldn't come to Tom's rescue every day. The ladies would figure out soon enough what I'd done, and anyway, I was in school most of the day. I glanced at Tom. He appeared absorbed in Janey Holstead's essay, unaware that nothing had been changed. I opened my mouth to tell him, then shut it.

This was one problem I was by gum going to solve myself.

Trouble was, I couldn't come up with a single lousy idea. After several days of serious thought, I knew what I wanted: for the ladies to back off—but to keep bringing food.

Those food offerings were making a big difference in my students. Some of my poorest scholars had begun to show signs of being able to learn, and it was dawning on me that hunger is no foundation for a good education. Still, if I let the ladies go on as they were now, Tom would either flee or—God forbid—give in and take one of them. Either way, the stream of casseroles and cookies would dry up.

What I needed was a way to control the crowd, but not to discourage them altogether.

I got so absorbed in the problem that finally my students noticed I wasn't paying them much attention. When they complained, I laid out the whole problem for them, including the part about keeping the food coming. They got that, all right, but no one seemed to have any notion how to pull it off, so I resumed the arithmetic lesson.

Tommy Colson didn't join us. He kept staring at the ceiling like maybe he was seeing some answers there. I almost held my breath. Tommy is no scholar, but he's smart enough—and he was motivated. I was pretty sure the ladies' offerings were the first decent meals he'd ever had.

All the kids charged out the door the minute I dismissed school. All but Tommy. He stayed in his seat, oblivious to everything, while I set the room to rights and laid things ready for the next morning. I was about to rouse him so I could leave, when his gaze came back from infinity and he broke into a broad grin.

"I got it, Teacher." He started talking, and when he was done, we were both grinning. I stuck out my hand, and we shook on it.

"Let's do it." We were nearly out the door before I started having second thoughts.

"Wait one cotton-pickin' minute, Tommy. We gotta think about this."

"It's a good plan," Tommy insisted.

"Yeah, sure. But we don't want to shut down the whole library. Or the whole town."

"Huh."

"No, sirree. We can't have word getting out our Librarian has some contagious disease—that's something catching, Tommy, like you suggested—because then no one at all would come to the library, and he'd have to leave anyway. No," I said, my mind starting to work, "what we need is . . ." I couldn't think of an answer.

"To make them think he needs feedin' but it ain't safe for them to come in," he finished for me. "Sumpun' 'at'd not hurt anybody but widders."

"Shingles?" I suggested.

"Mebbe." He agreed cautiously, but I could see he didn't like the idea. We'd both heard of people getting shingles who weren't so old.

"I got it!" Tommy announced again.

This time, he really did.

Less than a week later, I walked into the library during morning recess. Three baked-egg casseroles cooled on the windowsill, but there wasn't a grey hair in sight.

"Quiet this morning," I commented.

"Yes. As you can see, deliveries continue, but for some reason, none of the ladies wishes to linger."

"Interesting."

"Most. Those who ventured to speak offered their hopes that I would soon be feeling better. I was not," he added dryly, "aware that I had been ill."

"Oh?" I tried to preserve my air of innocence.

"Come, now, Alice. It is quite clear to me that you are in some measure behind this."

"Not me, Tom. Really, it wasn't me."

"Oh?" He made a small, almost imperceptible gesture toward the black silk mask in his pocket, and I hurried to add,

"Not all of it, anyway. It was Tommy Colson solved your problem."

"Oh? And what problem was that?"

For one awful moment I thought he actually wanted the widows around. Then I caught the twinkle in his eye.

"Seemed like you were a bit overrun with unwed ladies," I ventured. "A fellow might have had to pick one or leave town."

"And you feared I might leave. No, Alice, I'm not so easily frightened. I could have stopped them. But had I done so, the food would have stopped too. Just how did you manage?"

I explained. "So, Tommy just made up a sickness for you, one that only hurt single ladies of a certain age, just in case word got out beyond the ladies. And one that might, just maybe, get cured by good eating. Sometimes I think folks in this town'll believe anything."

He fixed me with a stern look. "It wasn't Tommy who spread the word, now was it?"

"Nope," I admitted.

"But Tommy thought of it?"

"Yep."

"I do wonder what gave him the idea," Tom mused.

"Well," I ventured, "I figured he kinda liked not being hungry. Maybe it even sharpened his wits a bit. He really didn't want to go back to bein' empty. Hunger is the mother of invention, they say."

"Seems that's not exactly the way I heard it," Tom said, "but I think it adequately answers my question."

THE NINJA LIBRARIAN AND THE GLORIOUS FOURTH

School was out for the summer, and my pupils were at loose ends. Well, at least the ones who were not hard at work pulling weeds and running errands for Ma and Pa. Seemed like my most interesting pupils mostly had nowhere to go and nothing to do, on account of their parents hadn't gotten around to noticing them. If they had parents. They did some fishing and squirrel hunting, girls and boys alike. There were plenty of wild girls around Skunk Corners, as hard to distinguish from the boys as I am. Difference was, around fourteen or so most decided to be girls and changed their ways. I couldn't see any future in it.

Anyway, once the fish were caught and the squirrels skinned, the young'uns with no one to boss them started gravitating back toward the school, out of habit, I suppose. They took to hangin' about in the yard, and then they took to hangin' about me.

"They're bored," Tom said when I complained. He didn't seem the least bit surprised either by their boredom or by their presence in my vicinity. "All winter you've given them something to do, and encouraged them to think. Now no one's doing either, and I imagine they have not yet learned to do so on their own."

"Well, I wish they'd take their boredom somewhere else! It's my holiday too, and I don't need 'em." I could say that because we were alone in the library, since Tom hadn't yet opened for business. Annoyed as I was, I wouldn't have said it in front of the youngsters.

Tom eyed me as I wandered from shelf to shelf, looking again for a book I cared to read, or one out of place that I could restore to order. He didn't say anything, but the Ninja Librarian can think powerful loud when he wants. I heard him just as clear as could be. He wanted me to do something with those kids.

It took me another week to be ready to listen. Then it wasn't Tom, so much as Tommy Colson, who made me change my attitude. I've a ridiculous soft spot for that piece of trouble, so when he came to me for help I just had to listen.

"It'll be the Fourth of July in just a couple of weeks, Teacher." I'd tried for a time to get the children to call me "Miss," but it didn't set well with them or me. We'd settled on "Teacher" as a long sight more respectful than "Big Al," which is how most folk call me.

"It's gonna be the Fourth," Tommy was saying, "and ain't nobody doin' a thing about it. I suppose a few of the fellows'll shoot up Tess's, like always. No fireworks, no parade, no picnic." He lingered on that last word, and I knew he felt the loss of the meals I'd been providing along with school. Seemed the widows around Skunk Corners weren't as easily fooled as we'd thought, because when school let out, the stream of cakes and casseroles coming to the library dried right up.

But I guess those ladies weren't smart enough to know the kids stayed hungry all summer, though I admit it was some better, what with hunting, and fishing, and stealing from their neighbors' gardens.

"Skunk Corners has never had a picnic or a parade," I pointed out.

"That ain't so!" Tommy argued. "Harry says when he was little, they had a parade and speeches and everything. And a picnic," he added, sticking to the essential point.

I'd never known that, but I've not been in Skunk Corners even three years, so there were things I'd never heard. I did know that if matters in town had gone downhill, Tommy's brother, Wild Harry Colson, and his pal Crazy Jake were likely responsible. At least partly. I'll admit they had some help when it came to mayhem. For all that, it was better here than where I'd come up.

"I think we oughta have a picnic," Tommy insisted.

"Uh-huh," I muttered, trying to turn back to my reading.

"So will ya' help us?"

I put the book down. "Help who, and with what?"

"Help me an' Peggy, Hank, and the rest make a real Fourth of July, with a picnic and all." He seemed surprised I had to ask.

"Now Tommy, how are we gonna do that? I can't cook. Can you?"

"Naw. We need real folk to do that. 'Sides, it wouldn't be much of a picnic unless everyone was there. So you gotta get the mayor and everyone to help. You *gotta*, Teacher."

I was all ready to tell him to go jump in Skunk Creek when I recollected what the Ninja Librarian had told me, or at least looked at me. Was this the job he thought I should take on?

"Okay, Tommy. I'll see what I can do."

He stared to whoop, and I held up a hand. "I'm making no promises. The mayor and all don't think so much of me, you know. They mightn't listen at all."

"You'll think of somethin', Teacher. I know it." Tommy raced off in high excitement, and I betook myself to the library to lay my problem before the man with the answers.

"So, as I see it," Tom said in his precise manner, "you need to persuade the town leaders this is a good idea."

"Sure," I muttered. "And how can I do that? They mostly don't think I'm worth much, you know."

"They thought enough of you to make you the teacher," he said.

I sighed at his innocence. "That's because there was no one else who could read and cipher. And would work for five dollars a month an' a room behind the school," I added.

He didn't argue with that. He just ignored it. "You will need a very thorough plan," he decided. "Present it in a business-like manner, and they will listen." Then he added, so low he probably didn't think I could hear, "Maybe."

"Tom?" I asked, not looking at him. "What does a real Fourth of July look like?"

"Have you never seen one?" I think it was the first time I had truly surprised him.

"I lived up yonder at Endoline until I came here. They never had any Fourth party, and you can bet on it."

Tom didn't look like he quite understood, but he nodded. "Then we'll start with some research." He studied the shelves, pulling down a book here and a book there. "You needn't read these cover to cover, but each one has a Fourth of July celebration in it somewhere. Maybe that will give you some ideas."

I glanced over the books. Story books, mostly. Seemed funny to me, but I trusted Tom.

I lugged those books to my room in the back of the schoolhouse, and set to reading. Two days later I came out, my belly empty and my head full. I headed first to the tea shop for a sandwich, which I wolfed in minutes before making my way to the library to deal with the ideas filling my head.

I walked in and waved a sheaf of notes at Tom. "I think I've got it! Everything for a real Fourth!" I read down the list: "Preaching, speeches, picnic, races or a baseball game, but I think we'd better stick with races, someone to recite the Declaration of Independence and maybe the Gettysburg Address, a parade of horses and wagons and all, some fights, and fireworks or a cannon."

"Fights?" Tom raised an eyebrow.

"Well, pretty much every one of those stories you gave me, 'cept Miss Alcott's, had someone fighting. I figure that's to commemorate the Revolutionary battles, right?"

"That's one way of looking at it." His tone was dry, and I got the idea maybe he didn't look at it quite that way. "Let's put this together into a plan and a schedule," Tom went on. "I suggest we leave out the fights, though."

"Leave out the preaching, too," I agreed. "We get enough fights, we don't need to schedule them, and no one pays any mind to Preacher Dawson."

The next afternoon I put on my best overalls, combed my hair, and walked into the mayor's office with a neatly-written plan. An hour later I emerged, dazed, and went in search of the children. It had taken me the first half-hour to convince the mayor I was serious, but in the end, he'd stood up and shaken my hand. We had ourselves an Independence Day party.

I found most of the school children, at least the ones I wanted, down by the creek. Fishing was done for the day, and most were swimming or wading. They crowded dripping about me as I announced the plan. "Foot-races in the morning, before it gets too hot. Picnic dinner at noon, everyone brings, everyone eats. Speeches after dinner. I had to say the Mayor could make one, but I made him agree Tess could make the other one." Tess was the proprietor of Two-Timin' Tess's Tavern.

"Bet Mr. Mayor Burton didn't like that," Tommy observed.

"Nope. But I said women should have a say, and she's the only one with nerve enough. Then," I went on, "Tommy will recite the Declaration of Independence, and Peggy will give the Gettysburg Address." The children just looked at me. "You have two weeks to learn them off by heart. The library has copies. And all of us are in charge of decorating the town up special." The children whooped, and then someone asked,

"What about fireworks? My Pa said a real Fourth party has fireworks and all."

I shook my head. "The Mayor wouldn't promise. Fireworks cost money. Maybe a bonfire."

A bonfire was enough to get the youngsters excited. We spent the next two weeks in a whirl of activity, though Tommy and Peggy missed a lot of the work as they struggled to learn their recitations. I knew Mayor Burton expected me to pick children of prominent people—his daughter, for example—but he'd not said so, and I'd no intention of doing things all his way.

Funny thing was, the more we got going with signs and banners and the like, the more folks joined in, until the whole town was excited about the party. For a while, I worried about the picnic, on account of I couldn't cook anything fit to share and Tommy couldn't bring anything either, but Tom assured me there'd be plenty. He seemed to know a lot about how things like this worked. He said no one would notice if we brought something or not.

When my young sprouts weren't building, decorating, and conning their lines, they were running, getting ready for the races. The boys, anyway. Of the girls, only Peggy had nerve enough— or any hope of staying with the boys. Eunice and Lily Rose were willing to tuck up their skirts and run, but they were too slow. Though I couldn't help thinking they might have caught those boys just fine if the race were a mile instead of a sprint. The girls were slow, but they could last.

We scrounged lumber from anyone who'd give us a board, stole some nails from the general store—just the ones on the floor, Hank promised—and built a platform for the speeches. I tested that carefully. It held me just fine, even when I jumped up and down, so I figured it would do for our speechifiers, even the

Mayor, as long as he didn't do any jumping around. I'm big, but not as big as he is.

July Third we spent all day putting up the platform, laying out the race courses, and draping the red, white and blue bunting the townswomen produced from somewhere. Even Tommy and Peggy were there, assuring me that they knew their speeches word perfect. I believed them, because they knew what would happen if they messed up. Plus, Tom had been coaching them, and he wouldn't let them get away with anything less than perfection.

By sundown on the Third the town square was ready. Pies and chickens and potato salads had been baked in every home where anyone knew how. And not one of my feral students had been in trouble for two weeks. That alone ought to convince the mayor it was worthwhile.

And I'd had more fun than I'd had since I was ten and had spent half the summer scheming to get my neighbor's goat into the parson's outhouse.

Tom was right, as usual.

But I wasn't going to tell him.

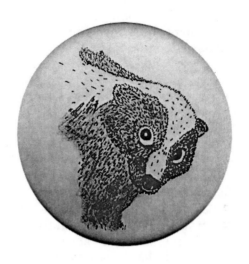

THE NINJA LIBRARIAN AND THE
GLORIOUS FOURTH, PART II

I have seldom enjoyed a meal as much as I did that Independence Day picnic. I sat with Tommy and Peggy, and it would be hard to say which of us ate the most. I'd never have believed kids their size could stow away that much food, though some of it may have ended up in pockets for later.

Across from us, the Ninja Librarian ate with a restraint I could scarcely imagine. Either they teach an awful sort of self-denial wherever he learned to be what he is, or he's a far better cook than I am.

Or maybe not all those widows had given up.

I was distracted from the thought by the appearance of another dish of potato salad. By the time we'd taken care of that, the mayor was up on the platform we'd built, and I napped a little while he ran on. An over-full stomach doesn't make for a particularly attentive listener—any more than does an empty stomach. Sometime when I wasn't half asleep, I'd have to think about that. Even the kids might have slept a bit, despite their excitement, because they'd run in the races before sitting down to lunch, and acquitted themselves right well—in the races as well as at the table.

When Peggy had lined up to run with all the boys, a fair number of people had laughed. But she just ignored them, hitched up her skirts until the bottoms of her bloomers showed above bare legs and bare feet, and kept her mind on the job. When they rounded the corner at the far end, we could all see that two runners had pulled well ahead of the others. Someone hollered that it was a two-man race, just about the time we all saw that one of those "men" was wearing bloomers. Things got a bit quieter all of a sudden, but that didn't seem to bother either runner.

When Peggy crossed the line right behind Tommy—and ahead of everyone else—I collected a comfortable sum from those who'd been sure no girl could ever beat any boy. I'd figured both Peggy and Tommy were used to running from angry farmers and housewives. They stirred up some feelings on their foraging expeditions time to time. Besides, most of the other boys were hampered by having parents who made them wear shoes. So I'd bet on Tommy and Peggy as a one-two deal.

Since bare feet were better for summer and races than winter and snow, I planned to use a bit of those winnings to buy Peggy and Tommy each a pair of shoes, come winter.

The men's race came off next, and they weren't much faster than the boys. I guessed Tommy could have beat most of them, and maybe Peggy could have, too. The men around Skunk Corners tend to do their running a-horseback.

Anyway, like I say, food and races and warm sunshine made sure we mostly dozed through the mayor's speech, but when Tess Noreen, owner of Two-Timin' Tess's Tavern, got up to give her speech, I came right awake. I was almost holding my breath, if you want to know, seeing as how she was my idea.

A sort of rumble and gasp went through the crowd. Murmurs of "a woman like that" and "how dare she?" came from the women, while the men made a noise more appreciative of what they saw, but not amounting to open admiration on account of the wives and respectable women all around them.

Tess acted as though she didn't notice a thing. She was dressed like she was for work, with maybe a bit more bosom showing than most of the women in town would've shown, but she wore it well, and the men noticed, like I said. Then the men realized the woman was going to give a speech, and their rumbles changed tone.

For a minute, it looked like there might be a ruckus, but Tom touched his napkin to his lips, stood up, and began to move through the crowd. Here and there, where someone seemed unwilling to let well enough alone, his hand drifted toward the bit of black silk in his breast pocket, and folks sort of subsided. Most everyone in Skunk Corners knows that's no handkerchief in his pocket. Even the folks who'd come in from farther out had heard about him, though they might not have believed all they'd heard.

When Tess had everyone's attention, she proceeded to deliver a wholly unexceptional speech on our glorious democracy, getting only a bit of a rumble from her Suffragist conclusion that "as women are people, capable of thinking, feeling, planning and yes, running a business, as well as a man, I find no reason we should not participate fully in this democratic state."

That brought a moment's stunned silence, until, led by Mrs. Herberts, who's run the tea shop all alone since her husband got himself killed by a bad horse, the women began to cheer. The men chimed in a bit belatedly, many following a good jab in the ribs from their wives, who seemed to have forgotten their objections to Tess's business and attire.

Tess sat down, and Mayor Burton stood up again. "And now, two of our fine Skunk Corners scholars will recite the Declaration of Independence and the Gettysburg Address."

Again the crowd rumbled when Tommy and Peggy stood up and made their way to the podium we'd built the day before. Tommy stepped up to look over the crowd, pale but resolute. The mayor looked at his daughter, clearly wondering why she was not up there, but she just shrugged. I don't think she minded. Marybeth knows her limitations.

After one scared look over the audience, Tommy opened his mouth and began to recite, and you could hear him clear to the back of the crowd.

"When, in the course of human events, it becomes necessary for one people . . . ." When he finished he sat down amid thunderous applause. He hadn't missed a single word or so much as stumbled.

Peggy stood up and, not waiting for the inevitable murmurs of disapproval, launched right into Lincoln's speech. You could hear her, too, right enough. Especially the part where she changed "all men are created equal" to "all people are created equal." Fortunately, no one seemed to know it was a change, and she carried on without showing the slightest sign she'd done anything odd. When she came to the end, thunderous applause broke out.

Peggy turned bright red and ran back to our table, where she hid behind me.

Thus far, the day was a perfect success. The children had been having a wonderful time, and had shown the grown folk that Skunk Corners could do this as well as anyone. We'd had races, speeches, and a picnic to remember. All that remained was the bonfire, but that would have to wait for evening.

But after the speeches, something changed.

Tess had begun serving at noon, her usual time, but she and her barkeep, Johnny, had been watching close and not letting any of the usual good-for-nothings get drunk. But someone else had less sense, or more greed, because by three or four in the afternoon, Crazy Jake, Wild Harry Colson, and a whole lot of out-of-town fellows were drunker than a prospector on a toot.

It was Tess and Peggy caused the trouble, in a manner of speaking. Some of those boys just couldn't stand the idea of women doing much of anything outside of what a man told her to do, and Cal Potts started shooting off his mouth about uppity women who wouldn't keep in their place. He's from Two-Bit, and probably only came for the drinking—and maybe for the fighting.

I didn't see the start of it, but the children told me about it. Seems Cal said Tess was no better'n she should be, which I figured was true enough and didn't upset anyone. But he added that no one but a bunch of sissies would have put up with her suffragist nonsense. Well, Tommy Colson heard that, and said it was Cal who was full of horse feathers, because look at Peggy and you could see girls were just as good as men, some of them. The kids told it to me that way, though I had a hunch it wasn't "horse feathers" Tommy accused Cal of being full of.

Anyway, that's when Cal told Tommy that Peg was on her way to being as bad as Tess, and—I had to get this from one of the children too little to understand—it was all on account of their no-good teacher who thought she was a man and was likely to come to no good end. I felt real bad about that. Not because I was insulted, but because Tommy suffered for it.

You see, that was when Tommy jumped Cal, who's twice his age and darn near twice his size. Of course Cal laid him out fast, and then Wild Harry got mad. Tommy's his little brother, and whatever else you might say about Harry, he understands family loyalty. It didn't even matter he probably agreed with Cal. No one was going to knock down his little brother and get away with it.

I got there just in time to see Harry jump over Tommy's prostrate body and sail into Cal.

"No one hits my baby brother, you low-down rotten sheep-lovin' son of a horse turd!"

I have to say, Harry had a more interesting line of insults than I'd have expected. Made me think, or would've if there'd been any time for thinking.

Where Harry jumps, Jake follows, and Cal has his pals, so before long the whole square was a mess of fighting men. It looked like a disastrous end to our party—just a matter of time before two long tables holding what pies and cakes we hadn't yet eaten got knocked over. I was debating joining the brawl, just to guard Tommy, who hadn't moved, when a white-haired figure appeared in the midst of it all.

Tom.

Ninja or no, I figured him for a goner when he started commanding those crazy louts to stop.

Cal and three of his pals stopped fighting with Harry and Jake, and turned on Tom. Harry and Jake knew better than to mess with the Ninja Librarian.

They just stood and watched. I swear I saw Harry grin when Tom pulled that black silk mask from his pocket and put it on.

By the time Cal reached him, Tom was set.

One strike and two kicks later, Cal and his pals were on the ground, and Tom stood, relaxed and not even panting, while the others decided if they would or they wouldn't.

Apparently they weren't too drunk to think, because they didn't, and the riot dissolved as quickly as it had started. Most of the rioters slunk away to the creek to wash up. A few lay on the ground and didn't get up.

The more peaceful folks began crawling from under tables and behind wagons.

The kids moved in on the pies and resumed feasting.

Tom looked around. "I believe that should clear up the matter."

The roar of the crowd—and a dipper of cold creek water—brought Tommy around. He sat up, a dazed grin on his face.

"Hey! There *were* fireworks! I saw them!"

Everyone laughed except Tom. He looked over the crowd and raised his voice again.

"Some among you said Skunk Corners could never pull off an Independence Day celebration where a family could come and have a good time. What say you now?"

A roar of laughter and agreement met the comment. It appeared that, once again, the Ninja Librarian had completely answered our questions.

THE NINJA LIBRARIAN AT SUMMER'S END

T he dog-days of August here in Skunk Corners must be about the worst time anywhere. Not even the bit of elevation we have over the searing valley protects us from the heat, and in late August the cooling breezes of fall were weeks away. In the afternoons you could hear the pinecones popping open in the heat, letting their seeds fly. Those might have been the trees that usually waited for a fire to open the cones. It was that hot.

I even caught the Ninja Librarian using that black silk of his to wipe his brow, rather than to mask his eyes. One day I came into the library and he was actually in his shirtsleeves. The natty frock-coat he wears all the time hung on the back of his chair.

As for me, it was so hot I sometimes traded my overalls for a skirt. Mostly I did it when no one could see me, then hiked the thing up to my knees so's I could cool off a bit. The ladies in town would've died before doing such a thing, but I could tell a lot of corsets were being left off. A mess of heavy fabric and whale bone like that must be awful hot, though you'd never catch me putting one on to find out. Mrs. Mayor Burton wouldn't leave hers off, not until she fainted twice in one week and Doc Thorpe insisted.

My pupils—I figured they were mine even if school wasn't keeping—spent most of their time down by the creek, which was shrinking up like it always did in summer. We still had enough of a swimming hole for the kids, but only just. I liked a larger hole I knew of a few miles up the creek. But the walk up there was near enough to kill in our August heat, so I didn't go too much.

It got so hot, all activity in Skunk Corners pretty much ground to a halt. It was too hot for work, and Tess was selling mostly beer and even ginger-beer. It was too hot for whiskey, and for our town, that's some kind of hot.

The only good thing was, with the kids unwilling to budge from the creek, they finally left me alone. Ones like Tommy Colson and Peggy Rossiter were at the swimming hole from sun-up to sun-down, but even Marybeth Burton, the Mayor's daughter, joined them afternoons, once she'd done her sewing—I think her mother was teaching her fancy embroidery—and practiced the piano. Others snuck away from weeding or other chores, knowing it was too hot for the grown folk to chase them.

And we watched the forest bake dry and waited for the weather to break.

The one cool place in town was the basement of the library, and before the heat wave was very old, Tom and I took to holing up there most days. We took turns going up to keep the library open. More people were reading since it was too hot to work, and we were finally checking out enough books that Tom could send for new ones. That gave us more work, sitting down in the basement cataloging the new books. I tried to read most of them at the same time, which slowed things up a bit.

Neither of us said it, but it was just as well I had this new work to do. After the Independence Day picnic, the kids who'd been keeping me busy had drifted off to the creek. I'd never have admitted it, but I was at loose ends. Of course, I had the new school year to plan for, and I claimed that as my excuse to be at the library so much. Maybe it was even partly true. After all, the more a teacher reads, the more she knows, and the better she can teach, right? Besides, like I said, Tom needed help with all the new books.

Skunk Corners had been baking for weeks, seemed like, when Tom brought me a pile of new books and a question.

The books were all about teaching—managing a schoolroom, keeping records, and things I'd never thought about, like teaching science and nature studies.

"What? You think I need help teaching?" Knowing how little I knew mostly just made me resent Tom's efforts to help. I still smarted over his success in teaching the children to read, even if he did insist he only convinced them to admit I'd already taught them. Maybe it was even true, but I still felt inadequate.

Tom refused to respond to my irritation. "Everyone can improve, Alice."

I thought the reply annoyingly noncommittal, and didn't give up my resentment. "Oh yeah? What about you, then?"

He smiled a little and held up a book. I read the title: "The Small Town Librarian."

"Huh. And the other part? Your, uh, other skills?" Then I held my breath. We'd never spoken of Tom's Ninja skills, beyond the statement he'd made the first day: "Don't worry about me. I am trained to kill."

"That's not something learned from books, and I have no teacher here. But," again that gentle smile, "I practice daily."

He did? When on earth did he do that? I'd never seen him at it, unless you counted the fights he'd had. But those'd been a lot less than daily. Then again, I'd never gotten to the library before he was up and breakfasting, so maybe he did it in the early morning. The *very* early morning.

Catch me working that hard before breakfast!

Then he came out with another question and I forgot all about his Ninja practice. "When does school start again?"

I shrugged. "I dunno."

"Who does, then?"

I shrugged again. "No one, I reckon."

"What about the School Board?"

"They've never said nothing since they hired me." I suspected there wasn't really any school board. Probably Mayor Burton and a couple of the men had just gotten together long enough to hire me.

Tom wasn't giving up. "How did you determine a starting date in previous years?"

A third shrug. The heat made me cranky, and I was trying to annoy him. "The first year, school was in session when I started. Mr. Bentley left in a hurry, though I never did get the rights of why."

"And last year?"

49

Another shrug, this time because I truly didn't know what to say. "It just started. One day a whole slew of kids showed up, so I started teaching them."

"Then I take it you and the children wait for a sign from the gods?" Tom's tone was drier than the dust in the street.

There didn't seem to be any answer to that. I just took up the pile of books he'd given me and headed home.

Soon's I got there, I regretted it. My room behind the school was hotter'n blazes, but I wasn't going back. I propped open the back door by my room and sat there on the top step with that skirt hiked up around my knees and sweated and read.

That afternoon I made my way down to the swimmin' hole at the creek. The children were pretty much all there, except poor Marybeth. The water was getting low, and turning a bit green. I got there just in time to see Tommy and Hank sail into each other. I let them exchange a few blows before I waded in and hauled them apart, holding one in each hand. I had to pick Tommy right up off the ground before he'd stop swinging at Hank.

I didn't bother asking why they were fighting. There didn't need to be any reason for fist fights at the hot, dry end of summer.

Once I'd settled those two, I went on up to my own swimmin' hole. Truth to tell, it wasn't much more than a puddle by then either, and probably not worth the hike. I sat in it anyhow and thought about Ninja Tom's question. About how I'd know when to start school. Maybe when the swimming holes went dry? But the thought of all of us sweltering in the schoolhouse didn't make me want to jump with joy.

I got back to town in time to break up a fight between Peggy and Marybeth. Even the Mayor's daughter seemed to have forgotten she was prim and proper, and was fighting like a boy, with fists, not with hair-pulling and name-calling the way girls mostly fight.

Tom saw me breaking up the next fight, this time between a couple of the little ones who I thought might be ready to start school this year. They were maybe six, and seemed fresh out of ideas for entertaining themselves. Tom looked at me and raised his eyebrows. I could tell what he was asking, as clearly as if he'd come up and said, "have you not enough information yet to determine a starting date for your school?"

But, well, I didn't. Maybe three fights in one day was telling me something, and maybe it wasn't. What I really wanted was to wait for the fall rains, or at the very least, for the heat to break. I knew the fall rains wouldn't likely start before October, even up here in the mountains. But we might get a thunderstorm that would break the heat and make it tolerable to be indoors.

The heat was worse than any I could remember. Of course, up in Endoline where I'd come up, it never did get this hot, and the thunderstorms came down on the mountains pretty often. Skunk Corners was closer to the valley, but still high enough we usually came in for a share.

Not this August. The only storms we'd seen for weeks had been fist fights. Counting the latest face-off between little Melly and Billy Jenkins, we'd had them from the six-year-olds right up to two toothless geezers who always sat on the porch of Johnson's Mercantile and argued about everything. Yesterday, seemed they'd gotten to arguing over the weather—if this was the hottest, driest summer ever, or if the one back when they were laying the rails up to Endoline and five men had died of the heat was worse—and they ended up exchanging blows. Tom had broken that one up, quite gently, really. For him.

Three days later, I figured out when to start school. That was the day I started in to clean up the schoolhouse, turning out all the cupboards and trying to get a line on who'd be my scholars for the year.

I'd already been to see Melly's—Amelia Greer's—parents, and also the Jenkinses. I made sure to bring up Billy's schooling when Crazy Jake wasn't around. Jake is Billy's uncle, and I didn't know how he felt about schooling, other than that he—Jake—hadn't had much.

But it wasn't any of that that told me I needed school to start. Not the dry swimming holes, not the kids' fights, not even having the school ready and the students enrolled. I added Billy and Melly to the primer class, and my oldest student, having turned twenty, decided she'd best put more time into finding a man and refused to come back, even to finish the Fifth Reader. Certainly it wasn't the heat ending that told me to start, because it didn't end.

What told me I'd better open the school was that I got into a fight with the Ninja Librarian.

I don't mean an argument, either. We'd had a few of those over the months since he came to Skunk Corners, but they didn't amount to much.

What happened was, Tom came and told me that if I wasn't going to run a school here in this town, I ought to go away and get a proper education myself. That's when I lost my head.

"Are you saying that I'm ignorant?" I said it just like I would have to any tough in Tess's.

"I am merely saying," he began in his quiet way, and I just up and jumped him.

I actually landed two blows before I flew out the schoolhouse door to land in the street. Since the dust on the street was several inches thick by then, my fall was well-cushioned and I was perfectly capable of hearing the words that followed me out the door:

"Does that completely answer your question?"

It answered a whole slew of them.

I opened the school the next day.

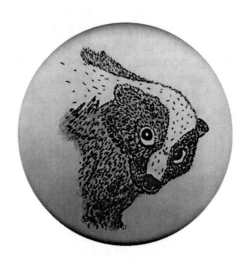

THE NINJA LIBRARIAN MEETS HIS MATCH

Summer vacation had ended in a puff of dust, the dust raised when I hit the street with a little help from the Ninja Librarian. With one quick flip he'd shown me not only that it was time to start school, but that I could use some more smarts. So I opened the school, but I wasn't sure what to do about my own ignorance.

I'd read the books Tom got for me. I'd been hoping for more stories as good as Mr. Stevenson's *Kidnapped* and *Treasure Island*, but *Classroom Management for the One-Room Schoolhouse* and *Nature Studies with Children* had proven to be of greater interest than I'd have thought. I was surely gong to make use of the suggestions about using older children to teach younger ones. Not Hank and Yance, of course, but it might be the only way to keep Tommy Colson and Peggy Rossiter out of trouble.

I wasn't quite as sure about *Nature Studies*. Didn't my pupils live smack in the middle of nature? Skunk Corners isn't exactly the big city. How much study did they need about bugs and plants? They all knew to avoid black widow spiders and poison oak, and they all knew—except maybe poor Marybeth Burton, the Mayor's daughter, who was being brought up to be a lady—which plants were good for a snack. I'd have to give some thought to that one.

September continued to be as hot and miserable as August. I took to starting school as soon after sun-up as we could all get there, so I could dismiss class early and the kids could still spend the hottest part of the afternoon in what was left of the creek.

There wasn't much water there now. While the kids moaned about the loss of their swimming hole, the adults in Skunk Corners worried about the springs drying up. We all got our water from Skunk Springs, and they'd never failed yet, but the flow into the cistern had slowed to scarcely more than a trickle. If we didn't get rain soon, we were all in trouble and no mistake. The muddy water holes in the creek wouldn't keep us supplied for long.

I found myself looking at Tom, waiting for him to offer a solution. I knew better, of course. What could even a Ninja Librarian do about a drought?

"Still no sign of rain?" he asked when I came to the library after school on the fifteenth of September. I shook my head, and we descended to the basement, the coolest spot in town. Or out of it, now that the creek was mostly dry.

"Is it always like this around here at this time of the year?"

"Naw." I paused to wipe the sweat from my face. "Most years we have thunder storms along through August and September, until the winter rains come along. They keep it a bit wetter and a lot cooler."

He looked so thoughtful at this news that I couldn't help asking, "Do you know some way to call up a storm?"

Tom laughed. "Alas, my training did not extend to the control of the weather."

"Rats," I said, and we both laughed.

Three days later the hot spell broke at last. Actually, "broke" seems an inadequate description. It shattered.

We'd been sweating through lessons in the Skunk Corners School ever since sun-up, and I was about ready to call lunch recess when it went dark. It was as though the sun was blotted out, dimming the glare that had seared our eyes for weeks. Naturally, we all ran to the windows to look out, and that was when the first clap of thunder hit.

I swear that all the storms we hadn't had for the last six weeks burst on us at once. The thunder rattled the windows, and the rain came down like a waterfall in spring. A few of the children shrieked at the thunder, but then, as one, we ran outside. Cool, damp air! Moments later, we were all dancing and laughing and shouting in the street.

It felt wonderful. Cool, clean rain poured over us. Most of the town was outside by now, though the grown ladies stayed under the eaves on their porches, not wanting to get all wet in public.

I saw Tom come out of the library in his shirtsleeves, and I splashed over to him, a big grin just about splitting my face.

"Isn't this just something like?" I hollered over the sound of the drumming rain. If he answered, it was drowned out by a crack of thunder so near it came right atop the lightning, and so loud it rattled the windows, to say nothing of shaking my gizzard.

A few minutes later I noticed that the puddles in the street were deeper than they had been, and seemed to be moving downhill toward the depot and tracks at the end of the street. As the water grew deeper and faster almost before our eyes, Tom let loose with a shout.

"Flood!" His normally quiet voice carried well enough to be heard over the rain. "Children! Into the library, NOW!"

I guess being a Ninja teaches some kind of force of will, because every one of my students turned and ran for the library at once. As the only brick building in Skunk Corners, the library stood the best chance of not being washed away in a flood. But if we didn't do something, not even the library would hold up.

As the students filed in, I nabbed Hank and Yance, my seventeen-year-old sixth reader students. "You two—get down the street and warn everyone. Tell anyone who can help to get up here. We've got to turn the flood!" I had no idea if such a thing was possible, but if we didn't try, surely the town would be swept away.

Tommy and Peggy tried to come, too, since they're in the fifth reader now, but they're only eleven, and I turned them firmly back. "You two are in charge here. Keep the little ones quiet and calm. No one leaves until Mr. Tom or I come back. You hear me?"

They nodded. Peg was so pale her freckles looked like spatters of paint on a clean wall. But the set of her chin told me those children would stay safe inside as long as the library stood.

I closed the door and ran after Tom. Hank and Yance were already coming back up the street with a crowd of men, and Tom was leading them upstream—as you might now say. I figured he was looking for the best place to turn the flood, but where that would be, I had no idea.

We all saw soon enough what had let the creek out of its course. A huge oak that overhung the swimming hole had fallen, undercut by the rushing water. It both blocked the path of the stream and created a weak spot for the water to leap the bank. It hadn't taken long for the stream, now a torrent a man couldn't stand against, to dig a new channel.

Tom stood still, surveying the situation. Several of the townsmen fidgeted beside him, gesticulating and arguing. Tom ignored them.

"We have two chances," he called to the gathering crowd. I noticed that, besides me, two other women had joined the volunteers: Tess Noreen, owner of Two-Timin' Tess's Tavern, and Tildy, the oldest and most sensible of the women who worked for Tess. They'd already kilted their skirts above their knees, and looked more capable than some of the men, especially Mayor Burton, who was wearing a suit and low shoes, and stood wringing his hands while Tom took charge.

"Half of you," Tom started to say "men" but caught sight of me and Tess and changed it. "Half of you folks get to work digging a channel up from the other side of this hole. Make a way for the water to get back in the right course."

Hank and Yance came panting up with a pile of picks and shovels, and Tess and Tildy and I were the first to grab hold. Tom was assigning others to get ropes on the tree and sent for the strongest horses in town. He wanted to shift that tree, but I didn't think even a Ninja could do that.

Finally Tom held up a pair of crosscut saws and called for volunteers. I probably wasn't the only one who thought he'd gone mad, but four men stepped forward, tough loggers who'd been in Tess's when the flood started. They were dressed for work, right down to their cork boots, but even so—that stream wasn't any pretty mountain creek anymore, but a wild flood that could sweep a man away. If that happened, they'd be fishing his body out of the Bay a hundred miles and more downstream.

After that, I didn't look anymore, but concentrated on digging. Maybe those fellows could cut the tree and make a path for the water, and maybe they couldn't. But we had a stream bank to cut through.

The tree blocked a lot of the stream—well, that was the problem, wasn't it?—but we still stood knee deep in water and muck to start on the channel, Tess and Tildy and me. Half a dozen men were spread out along the path, digging like machines, and two more were working from the upstream end, an even wetter job than mine. While I swung that mattock, Tess and Tildy dragged away the earth I loosened.

Sometime along there the rain let up, and you might think that would have solved the problem. But a mountain flood doesn't come from one spot, and there was still plenty of water draining off the high places. Given how fast the water had come up, I thought it had started raining sooner up there, too.

The men who'd gone for the horses reported that the street was knee deep on a plow horse, and the railroad workers were building a pile of sandbags to protect the depot. It stood across the end of the street, in the greatest danger of washing away.

Trouble was, we had the root end of the tree. If they could've pulled from across the steam, they might've stood a better chance of moving it, but when the water broke through, they'd be trapped against the hill. It was pretty clear to me that the tree wasn't going anywhere, but our diversion channel, as Tom called it, was.

Rebecca Douglass

Before we broke through, though, the sawyers out on the tree gave a shout. They'd cut through, and before they'd started cutting, they'd gotten ropes on the top half of that tree. So now, as they scrambled back down the trunk to solid ground—or what passed for it under the circumstances—the farmers hitched up those massive horses and started to walk downstream.

I jumped out of the stream with the ladies right behind me, and found Tom next to me, shovel in hand. I don't know why I was surprised to find he had power and skill with a muck-stick, because surely I'd seen his strength when he fought. But he made that look so easy, I'd never thought about it, and he did look sort of small and mild.

Right then, two things happened at once. That huge hunk of tree began to move—and water found our channel. In seconds, it was flowing hard and carving the banks deeper and wider.

"Git back!" Tess yelled, and we all jumped back. All but Tom. He was between me and Tess, and I'd naturally turned when she yelled, so I saw the branch knock him off his feet. He fell right into that stream, and I didn't waste any time yelling. I dove for his leg as he went over, got hold of a foot, and hung on like grim death.

The current was doing its best to pull me in after him when I felt hands on my own ankles and I was pulled back an inch at a time. I concentrated on hanging onto Tom. A dozen hands reached for him when we got close enough to shore, and I guess folks in Skunk Corners know what they owe our Ninja librarian, because they hauled him right out.

Tess let go my ankles and started pounding the water from Tom. Someone helped me to my feet, and I was on my way to his side when Doc Thorpe pushed us both aside. Doc sat Tom up, and I darn near went all girly and fainted, because his face was a mess of blood and mud. But he was breathing, coughing and sputtering out the water he'd swallowed.

He was still unconscious, though, and that scared me. Doc called for help to help carry him farther from the stream, which was carving those new banks back toward us fast. Men were working to block up the path the water had cut into town, but I stepped up to help carry the librarian.

We hauled that Ninja—Doc and me and Hank and Yance—straight down the wet street to Tess's. There we laid him out on the bar. I'd've taken him to the library, but remembered the children were there. Someone brought clean water, and when Doc had washed away the blood, the gash on Tom's forehead didn't look so bad.

"I don't think there's much damage," Doc said. "It's a nasty cut, but he's got a hard skull."

Tess offered the smelling salts she kept behind the bar, and Doc held the bottle under Tom's nose. His eyes popped open and he sat up, coughing and—I swear it—cussing. Doc had to grab him so he wouldn't fall over, but in a minute he was himself, more or less.

Tom looked around, took in his surroundings, and raised his eyebrows. Rather, he started to, until he felt that gash in his forehead. He reached up a hand, felt the blood and swelling, and looked right at me, as though I had all the answers.

"Alice? What happened?"

Tess saved me having to answer, telling him in a few words.

"So Al here grabbed your foot and I reckon saved your life," she concluded.

I found my voice and added, "And Tess and Tildy grabbed *my* feet and saved us both, or I reckon we'd be somewhere down the mountain." And dead, I didn't have to add.

Doc laughed. "Looks like you met your match this time, Ninja Tom."

I held my breath and looked at Tom, not sure how he'd react to that suggestion. He looked a bit pained, but I couldn't tell if it was because of Doc's comment or the lump on his head. Then Hank and Yance spoke in unison.

"Does that completely answer your question, Mr. Tom?"

I'll give him credit. The Ninja Librarian can take it when the joke's on him.

THE NINJA LIBRARIAN AND THE
HEADLESS HORSEMAN

F all doesn't come to Skunk Corners the way they say it does elsewhere. There's no burst of colorful leaves on the trees. Mostly around here it's Live Oak and Digger Pines, which stay greenish most all the time. But along about October there come some days when the air feels extra clean and the sky's a different shade of blue. You have to pay attention to see autumn around here.

We were having that sort of fall weather, with just a hint of chill in the wind, when I first heard the rumors. Since I heard it first among the littlest kids, I figured it for a story the big ones had made up to scare them. Way I see it, life is scary enough for most little folks around the Corners, so before I started afternoon lessons, I set out to put things straight.

"Look here, you big kids. I guess some of you've been making up stories to tell the little 'uns. Trying to scare them on account of Halloween coming up. Now I've got Melly and Billy crying about some headless horseman they think is gonna get them." I snorted. "I knew I shouldn't've given you Washington Irving to read, Tommy Colson. But if you've no sense, I thought at least you had a bit more imagination than just to serve up an old story like that."

Tommy is no good at rules, so he piped right up without raising his hand. "I never, Teacher. Honest. Peggy told us all," he added.

Surprised he'd rat on a friend, I turned to Peggy.

"I didn't make it up," Peggy said. "My brother saw him. The headless rider, I mean."

"Anyway," sniffed Billy, "I'd already heard afore I come to school. Uncle Jake told Pa about it." I'd forgotten Crazy Jake was Billy's uncle. I wasn't sure what it signified, but probably nothing good. I couldn't put my finger on Peggy's brother, though.

At this point, half a dozen other children chimed in that they'd heard this or that relation claim they'd seen this headless horseman. Since all the sightings had been late at night, just about closing time at Two-Timin' Tess's Tavern, I didn't take the reports too seriously.

Only, Sarah swore her Pa never went to Tess's, and he'd seen the thing on his way home from working the late shift at the rail yard.

Finally, just to shut them up and in hopes of returning their minds to the contemplation of arithmetic and geography, I struck a deal.

"Look here. I'll keep a watch out for a night or two, see if there's anything in this. Now, Janey, give me the nine-times table."

That, I told myself while Janey chanted numbers, would be the end of that.

And, for a night or two, it seemed I was right. I heard more talk down at Tess's, where I drink tea from a whiskey glass, but my research turned up nothing. Each night I sat up late reading, out in the schoolroom where I could see the main street. The schoolhouse is at one end of the street, where it narrows to the track that leads on up to Endoline. The railroad depot sits at the other end. Given the size of Skunk Corners, I had a pretty good view of the whole town. No horse could pass without me hearing, and anytime I heard hooves, I closed the cover on the lamp and watched.

Everyone I saw ride in or out, even at closing time, appeared to wear his head in the accustomed spot.

So I told the kids there wasn't anything in it, and didn't mention that no one else had claimed any sightings those two nights either. If a couple of the older kids knew that, they had brains enough to keep it to themselves.

I talked it over with Tom, too. The Ninja Librarian had heard the rumors, of course. He agreed with my assessment of the most probable cause—bad whiskey and uncontrolled imaginations—but didn't know how to explain Sarah's Pa. Tom confirmed that he wasn't a drinking man, but opined that fatigue could have a similar effect, as Sarah's Pa worked all day on the farm before going to the railroad yard.

He'd been to see Tess, who admitted she'd been getting whiskey from a new fellow, the usual source having suffered a setback when a fire got out of hand at his still, but he was back in business now, so she'd be serving the usual from here on out.

That night I allowed myself to doze over the Sixth Reader, out of which I was preparing the next day's lesson. Out of my twenty-threee students, four were in the Sixth Reader. Two of them had been there since before I was the teacher. Two more—Tommy and Peggy—had worked through the Second, Third, and Fourth after Tom's lessons last spring. They'd finished the Fifth Reader just the previous week. It made for interesting lessons.

It was a marvel to me how those kids had started to learn once Tom had told them they could. Well, that and getting a full belly. I wasn't sure which made the biggest difference, but the combination worked wonders. Peggy and Tommy weren't the only students who'd been making rapid progress, though they were moving the fastest.

So there I was, nodding over the Sixth Reader, when the sound of hooves woke me. Galloping hooves.

It took me a moment to wake up enough to dim the lantern, and by the time I reached the window, the rider was too far past to see him clearly. But even from the far end of the street I could tell there was something odd about his shape.

The rider paused in front of Tess's, the horse reared, and a whinny drifted back to me. When the front hooves hit the ground again, the animal took off at a run, swerving past the depot at the other end of town. I'd hoped he'd ride back past me so I could get a better view, but he vanished into the dark.

Next morning, I ambled on over to the library before school time. Out of habit, I let myself in the back door without knocking, only wondering when it was too late if I might catch the Ninja Librarian in his nightshirt.

Half of me hoped not, and half wondered what a Ninja slept in.

Maybe Ninjas don't sleep. At any rate, Tom was dressed and eating his modest breakfast when I came in. He looked up and smiled. It's one of Tom's more aggravating traits that no matter when and how I appear in his rooms he never seems the least bit startled. He must have ears like a cat—I'm quiet, but I know no one's perfect—and I guess maybe he's trained not to react, too.

Anyway, I sat down where he indicated and poured myself a cup of what I assumed to be coffee.

"I suppose you know why I'm here." I took a sip from my cup. Tea. I made a face and took another sip.

"I would imagine it has something to do with that rather curious equestrian who's been, ah, haunting Skunk Corners of late."

Haunting. Had that been a fancy way of saying he was hanging about, or was Tom suggesting we had a real ha'nt?

"Like I said the other day, I was mostly inclined to think the young 'uns were making up stories for Halloween," I said. "Or that Tess's whiskey was bad."

"But?" Tom prompted.

"But I saw him last night. Or saw something queer, anyhow," I amended. Tom is a stickler for accuracy.

"Likewise," was his next astonishing utterance. "I believe it is time we did something, would you not agree?"

By the time school started, we had us a plan, and I could hardly wait. Worst was not telling the children, some of whom seemed rather pale that morning, and more of whom could not sit still. Of course, what could I tell them? We didn't know what we'd find when we put our plan into action. We just knew that when we were done there'd be no mystery—and no more frightened children. Or adults.

As it turned out, I had to hold my peace for three days. We didn't expect the rider back the first night—he never had come two nights in a row—but he didn't come the next, either. Tom and I spend a long, cold, dull night lying in wait, and I was pretty crabby the next day in school.

I felt kind of bad when I made Marybeth Burton cry. It's not her fault she's stupid.

I locked up the school after the last pupil went home, and took a long nap. I had no intention of dozing off tonight and missing the fun.

Midnight found me and Tom hunkered down in the shadows between Two-Timin' Tess's saloon and the bank. It always had aggravated the banker that the tavern was next door. Didn't stop him from drinking there, though, nor from banking Tess's money.

There we sat, trying not to freeze, or fall asleep, or fall asleep and freeze, as that chill fall wind I mentioned was out in full force.

Everything was in place, and all we needed was that headless horseman.

Just about the time I couldn't stand it any longer, we heard hoof beats. At first they were slow, and so far distant I could barely hear them. Then they picked up speed, so that by the time the rider came into sight out past the schoolhouse he was moving at a good clip.

"Tom!" I hissed. "That ain't him!" Even at that distance, I could see the rider had a head, right where it ought to be.

"Wait." Tom murmured back, as the horse drew closer. Before the horse passed the school, the rider's head disappeared. Just like that, and so sudden I almost forgot to do my part. I scrambled to my feet a beat or two after Tom.

Like the other time, the horse drew up in front of the saloon, reared, and let loose a whinny that got everyone's attention.

This time, when his forefeet hit the ground, I was there. I planted myself smack in front of the beast, reached up, and grabbed the bridle as he came down.

Now, I like horses and they mostly like me, but I'll not deny it took nerve to do that. However many heads the rider did or didn't have, a horse is a large beast and can do some damage if it's of a mind to. Why, I read that back in olden times, when knights ran around in armor and all, they trained their horses to kill.

So when I reached for that bridle, I made sure I caught it, and I made sure I held on. Only when that was taken care of did I look at the rider.

At first glance he was sure enough headless. But when I took a closer look, he seemed awfully odd-shaped, and I saw in a flash he'd just pulled a cloak up to cover his head, which he'd hunched down as far as he could. It wouldn't have fooled a child for two minutes, but he'd never stopped long enough for anyone to get a good look. Besides, he'd made sure to come late enough that most witnesses were pretty well oiled, which meant they weren't well situated to think things through.

All this took only a moment, and could be seen even by moonlight. Along about then, Tess stepped up on one side with a lantern, Crazy Jake and Wild Harry on the other. Well, that took care of my first guess as to the identification of the jokester.

Whoever it was, he didn't want to uncover and go quietly. Somewhat hampered by his cloak, he tried to launch himself at Tom. You'd've thought the sight of that Ninja mask would have given him pause, but Tom was in the shadows so maybe he didn't see.

Whatever he was thinking, the rider started to leap, and Tom just reached out and grabbed his hand and sort of helped him along a bit. By the time the big bold rider was sprawled in the dust on his face—which was back out from its hiding place—Jake and Harry were on him. They pulled him to his feet and Tess held up the lantern.

"Cal Potts," she said in disgust. "I might have known. Thought you could make monkeys of us all, did you?"

Cal Potts spat dirt and flinched when Jake pulled his arms a little tighter behind him. "That's too easy," he sneered.

Tom had disappeared, reappearing now with another struggling captive, Cal's main side-kick, a low-life whose name I never bother to remember. The man had brought a crowbar, which was now in Tom's hand, the one that wasn't twisting the prisoner's arms up behind him.

"I caught this one trying to break into the bank," Tom said, his tone of mild reproof much what he'd use on a child sneaking a book from the library.

Tess took a good look and chuckled in a way that made my hair stand up.

"Well, now, I reckon that completely answers my question, Mister Librarian."

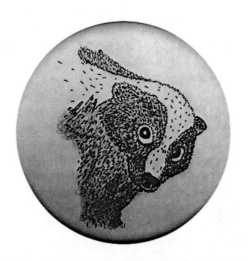

THE NINJA LIBRARIAN AND THE MISSING BOOKS

W hen the would-be bank robbers from Two-Bit had been shipped off to the sheriff over in Lupine, things should've been quiet in Skunk Corners. And they mostly were, if you didn't count Crazy Jake Jenkins and Wild Harry Colson getting drunk one Saturday night and getting into a fight. That was common enough, but this time they did it in the street, where they startled a team pulling a wagonload of turnips through town to the train depot.

Once we had the turnips cleared up—most went back to the irate farmer, though some likely made their way inside the shirts and jackets of certain of my students—things went back to being quiet. The next night, Jake and Harry got drunk and pledged their eternal friendship, and Tess had to stop them cutting their wrists wide open so they could be blood brothers.

Not long back, I'd've said to let 'em bleed. But they'd helped nail Cal Potts and his sidekick in their bank-robbing scheme, so I helped Tess bind their wounds.

It was only a couple of days later that Tom told me of the missing books down at the library.

I shrugged. "Books've been going missing from here for years. Who knows when they went?"

"I completed an inventory last month. Someone is taking books. Not last year, but right now."

I thought about that. "So what will you do about it?"

"When I know who is taking them, I shall know the answer to that."

I was pretty busy just then, so I didn't think any more about it. I mean, if the Ninja Librarian can't find who's stealing his books, I'm not likely to do much better. Besides, my sixth-reader students were running me ragged. They wanted me to teach them everything *right now*, from geometry to geology—that latter, I suspect, so that they could prospect for gold. The latest, though, was the idea they'd gotten that they should write a play and the whole school put it on.

I tried to convince them to concentrate on arithmetic, but they were stuck on their idea. It appeared I wasn't to have any say. Instead, my job, apparently, was to advise them and edit and, of course, to direct the play when it was written. My best hope was that they'd be off on a new tangent before we reached that point.

There was some hope of that. Tommy Colson and Peggy Rossiter were awful prone to take an idea and stick to it, the way they had with the Independence

Day party last summer. But this time they were trying to drag along Hank, who'd been in the Sixth Reader for three years, and Yance, who'd been there for four, and was pushing eighteen. Those boys struggled, and I suspected that Mr. Bentley, the teacher whose abrupt departure had left me in charge of the school more'n two years back, had put them in the top class due to their age, not their abilities.

Peg didn't care. "Way it'll work," she explained, "is we each write one act, and Tommy an' me'll put it all together."

"Tommy and I," I corrected.

"Naw, not you, Teacher. Me," Peggy insisted. I thought she'd missed my point altogether, until I saw the hint of a smile. Peggy was getting as bad as Tommy, I swear.

I sighed and gave up. "Fine. You and Tommy put it together. And I'll go back to setting lessons for the little kids."

"*And* you help us put the play on," Peggy clarified. "We've never seen one."

"Me neither." I hoped this confession would dim their enthusiasm a trifle.

"You ain't?" Peggy peered at me, disbelieving.

"Well, where do you reckon the nearest place might be to see a play?"

Peggy and Tommy looked at each other.

"I dunno," Tommy shrugged. "Down to the Coast?"

"Maybe a mite closer. But not in these hills."

"Yeah, but ain't you never been out of the hills? Yer a teacher!"

I wondered what they thought it took to be a teacher. "Nope. So I don't see as how I can help."

"Well," Tommy said after a moment's reflection on this revelation, "you always say if you don't know something, go to the library."

Right.

When I got to the library, Tom was shelving books, and I swear I heard him humming to himself as he did it. I listened, wondering what sort of strange music a Ninja would hum, but it sounded to me pretty much like "Buffalo Gals."

"Good afternoon, Alice." He stopped humming to greet me. "How are the young thespians today?"

"The what?" I've been trying to get used to admitting I don't know everything. I have to maintain my authority with the kids, so I don't usually let on to them. But Tom has a way of looking at me and raising his eyebrows that says he knows darn well I'm faking it.

"Thespians," Tom repeated. "Actors. From the Greek playwright Thespis, who is supposed to have invented the Greek tragedy."

"Never mind." I wasn't in the mood for a lesson in Greek. The 'young thespians' were the reason I was there, but the thought made me so cranky I changed the subject.

"Found out who's stealing your books?"

"Well, now, that's an interesting question," Tom evaded. "Let's just say I have a pretty good idea."

"What are you going to do about it?" Part of me kind of hoped he planned to kick them out. Literally. It'd been a while since there'd been any excitement at the library.

I was doomed to disappointment.

"Nothing, for now at least," was his unsatisfying response.

"Nothing? Yer just gonna let them mosey in and swipe the books?" My disbelief took my proper speech with it.

"Well, you see," he said, "they bring them back."

I was getting more and more bewildered. "They bring them back? So they aren't stealing?"

"Right. They bring them back, and then they take others."

Huh? That sounded an awful lot like, well, "that's just borrowing! Which is what the library's here for!"

"Right. Except these borrowers don't care to fill out a library card."

"Why ever not?" I began, then stopped, and the red crept up my face in a scalding wave.

"Why don't you tell me?" Tom asked gently. "Why would someone borrow books on the sly?"

"I don't!" I protested, realizing too late I'd been tricked into a confession.

"Not now," he agreed. "But you did."

I did. Right up until the Ninja Librarian moved in and I couldn't get away with it anymore.

No. Until the Ninja Librarian had taught me to be proud of my brains. The brains which were finally starting to work again.

"So someone is trying to hide the fact that they can read? Who?"

"Something like that," Tom agreed. "Now, what can I do for you?" The subject, apparently, was closed.

"Oh, I'm just browsing," I said, trying to remember if there were any books on plays, and if so, where I might find them. Naturally, I got distracted, and ended up carting off a half-dozen books, none of which had anything to do with writing or directing plays. But I had a great idea for a new area of study for the Skunk Corners students.

Over the next week, while my Sixth Reader students struggled with playwriting, I alternated between reading about the wonders of steam and wondering what was going on at the library. Tom still refused to say any more about the matter. Along about Wednesday I got the notion of figuring out for myself what books were going missing, and what was coming back without going past the desk.

My best idea was that someone was reading something they were ashamed of. That suggested either Preacher Dawson was reading dime novels, or just about anyone else in town was reading religious stuff. But nothing seemed missing from either category.

And what of my studies in drama? I completely forgot about them in my excitement over the books on steam power and my puzzlement over Tom's clandestine customers. Until I got hold of those books, I'd never thought to wonder how a steam engine worked. I had assumed it was a mystical process far beyond my simple understanding. But now, reading the books I'd taken from the library, I began to imagine actually building such an engine. An idea began to take shape in my mind.

I almost forgot about Tom's problem, until one night when, long past closing time, I found I absolutely had to have more information about the history and development of the locomotive. I didn't want to disturb Tom, so I used my key and let myself in the front, rather than the rear, of the library. I pushed open the door and froze, my foot half over the threshold. Though the room should have been dark and still, a lamp glowed on one of the tables. Perched on the hard chairs, hunched together over an open book, were Crazy Jake Jenkins and Wild Harry Colson. Next to them, erect and calm, sat Ninja Tom.

All three swiveled to look at me, the boys with faces reflecting a mixture of—what? Guilt and shame? Anger? I braced myself for an attack, certain that whatever they were up to, the boys wouldn't want me seeing them.

But Tom smiled and waved me over. "Ah, Alice. I believe you may be the very thing we require."

I stared at him until he went on. "The boys here are learning to read. You are a teacher. Perhaps you could help?" His explanation left me even more confused. Crazy Jake and Wild Harry were learning to read? Astonished they would admit they didn't know, I was even more astonished to find they cared. And wouldn't they kill me for knowing? I'm not afraid of the boys, precisely, but I didn't care to have the pair of them after me, either.

"Please, Teacher?" Wild Harry turned on me exactly the same pleading eyes his little brother used, and it occurred to me that maybe he felt silly, Tommy knowing more than he did.

I sat down in a daze. Harry had to have some brains, given Tommy's smarts, but was Jake anything other than Crazy?

I asked them to read, and listened to their struggles to wrestle meaning from the first primer, all the while wanting to ask them why. Why, after twenty-odd years, did they suddenly want to read, and why did they need to keep it secret? Well, big, tough guys could run into trouble if other toughs found them learning "A is for Apple" from a primer meant for six-year-olds. Plus, they'd been squawking ever since I came to Skunk Corners about how learnin' was for girls and sissies. Maybe that'd been to cover their shame at not knowing how to read.

My head was swimming, but I've been teaching long enough to go through the motions even when my brain's shot to bits. Crazy Jake looked pretty pleased with himself when he finished his sentence, but Wild Harry looked disgusted.

"This stuff ain't fit fer a growed man to read," he said. "You, Al, you find us somethin' thet ain't so babyish, hear?"

I heard, all right. But I gave him my best teacher glare, and put him right back where he belonged. "You just study up so you can read this baby stuff, and I'll give you something worth your while. Maybe you can learn to read half as well as Tommy, hey?"

"I'll read ten times better'n thet pipsqueak," Harry said, so fiercely that I knew I'd been right about why he'd suddenly needed to "get some schooling." And where Harry went, Jake followed.

I hadn't forgotten what I came for, and I set those boys a lesson so I could get the book I wanted. Tom had vanished back into his rooms, but I had a hunch he knew what was going on out front just the same. My hunch was confirmed when I pulled the book from the shelf, and he called from the back, "don't forget to sign that out, Alice."

"I won't! I never steal books!"

"Anymore," Harry snickered. While I filled out the card, he picked up the book and flipped through it. He was so absorbed that he kept on studying the book and its engravings when Jake went back to reading three-letter words for me. Finally Harry looked up.

"I want to read this. And I want to build one."

All of us stopped what we were doing and looked at him.

"What?" Jake and I chorused.

"What is it you wish to build, Harry?" Tom asked, never losing his grip on the complete sentence.

Harry held up the book. "One of these. A steam engine. How soon can I read this, Al?"

I tried to look as firm and confident as the Ninja Librarian. "That depends on you. How hard are you willing to work?"

"I can do it," Harry insisted, though without quite answering my question.

I glanced at Tom.

"I think, Alice, that this might be just what you need, don't you?"

That's when it came to me. It *was* what I needed. Once again, I'd found the answer at the library—though not to the question I'd come in with.

"Very well, boys." I figured Jake might as well be in on this from the start, as he'd surely be by the end. "I'll teach you to read this—and you'll help my students build a steam engine."

"Huh?" It was Harry's turn to be bewildered.

"Yup. Harry, you have to get Tommy to think steam and leave his play-writing alone. Then we build an engine and—" I stopped. And use it for what?

"And use it to pump water for the library and school," Tom concluded. "Hot water."

I heard the wistfulness in that last. It sounded like I'd answered more questions than I'd thought of asking.

THE NINJA LIBRARIAN BLOWS UP

Weeks had gone by since the last excitement in Skunk Corners and things were getting tedious. Oh, there were the usual Saturday night fights out front of Two-Timin' Tess's Tavern, but nothing that rose to a level you could call interesting.

I set lessons and my students learned. No one pretended to be stupid now. Even Hank and Yance showed signs they might finish the Sixth Reader before their hair turned gray.

They all did so well I'd started using the lessons I read about in *Nature Studies for Children*, and to my surprise we all learned a thing or two. The writer of that book knew more about the world, in a general way, than I'd imagined there was to learn. He didn't try to teach us what we all knew—the little things about our own mountains, what to eat and what to avoid and all—but more about the systems. Where the water and weather came from and where they went. That sort of thing.

After classes were over and the library closed for the night, I'd go knock on Tom's door, and he'd let me in and I'd teach Wild Harry Colson and Crazy Jake Jenkins to read. We were still sneaking around, though I never did get clear if they were embarrassed because they had always mocked learning and now they were trying to get some, or because they didn't already know how.

No matter. They were learning, and I tell you, once those boys decided they wanted to learn, I mostly just had to point them in the right direction and get out of the way.

Still later, after the guys had gone off to Tess's to practice reading the labels on the whiskey bottles, I took some lessons of my own.

When I'd been teaching Jake and Harry for a few weeks, I finally talked myself into it. If they could ask to learn to read, I could ask Tom to teach me to fight. Now, there are plenty who'd say I don't need any teaching about fighting. That I fight just fine, and anyway a lady shouldn't. But no one called "Big Al" by all the town is a lady, and I wanted to know.

See, our librarian doesn't know just any old sort of fighting. He wouldn't teach me to be a Ninja—he said that wasn't his decision to make, whatever that meant—but he would teach me to fight like one, at least a little bit. To be sure, it didn't feel like fighting to me. He hadn't taught me any kicks or punches, just ways to stand and breathe. I'd have complained, but somehow I couldn't bring myself to. Ninja Tom had already dumped me on my back in the street once for being a fool. I didn't need to repeat that lesson.

So I taught my young and not-so-young students, and stood and breathed, and the fall crept on towards winter. All summer we'd headed to the library basement because it was the coolest place in town. Now it seemed to be the warmest place in town, and I puzzled some over that.

I had to break the ice on the water bucket in the schoolroom every morning, and build up the fire before the children came. Some looked downright blue when they got in, and I worried. How would Tommy and Peggy, not to mention little ones like Crazy Jake's nephew, Billy Jenkins, make it to school when the snow started to fly? I'd meant to use my winnings from the races on the Fourth to buy them shoes, but it'd gone to feeding several of the children, not to mention myself, all summer. My salary only got paid when school was in session.

At least I could make sure the school was warm. Saturdays I got the bigger children to help me build up the woodpile, so's I didn't have to skimp on the fires. We scoured the forest for dead wood so it didn't have to season. Next summer, I vowed, we'd build the world's biggest woodpile behind the school.

There was just one other thing we spent our time on.

There was the steam engine.

With a little help from Harry and Jake, I'd managed to deflect Tommy and Peggy from theater to engine-building, and they spend all their spare minutes poring over the books and plans I'd found. This was one place Hank and Yance could keep up with their younger and smarter classmates, because those boys were fascinated by the diagrams, and if they struggled over the reading, they seemed to grasp how the plans worked without any effort at all.

By the time Thanksgiving came around, Crazy Jake and Wild Harry Colson were able to read the books

on steam engines, and our evening lessons took on a
new twist. Those boys had rejected math when I'd
suggested once before that they might want to learn,
but now they had a use for it. Seems it takes some
math to make a steam engine work. So they learned
figures, and I studied geometry one page ahead of
Tommy and Peggy.

And gradually we were developing a design, one
that would build a steam powered water heater and
pump.

When Thanksgiving came, we had a dinner at the
school that left us all groaning. Tess had arranged it,
and provided most of the food, but each of us
managed to bring something, even if it was only a few
apples. I provided the firewood. Nothing I cook is fit
to share with company. Not all my students were
there, of course, just the ones who would find no feast
at home, and maybe a couple of others who couldn't
pass up a party.

The younger children had gone home, and Tess
and her girls headed back to the Tavern. Crazy Jake
and Wild Harry Colson were about to follow when I
stopped them. They came back and sat down,
reluctant but willing to humor me. Tommy and
Peggy already had the plans out, and Hank and Yance
bent over them. Jake looked at Tom, who appeared to
be snoozing by the stove.

"What about him?"

"He has an interest in the project. I'm sure he'll
speak up if he has anything to add." I wasn't going to
bet the Ninja Librarian was truly sleeping. To the rest
of the kids, I added, "I've asked Jake and Harry to
give us a hand with the project."

"What do they know about steam engines?"
Tommy clearly didn't want to share.

"As much as you do." I could see the kids didn't believe me, but time would cure that. Besides, by the time I'd finished saying it, all six heads were bent over the plans, and they'd forgotten all about me. I went and sat down by Tom, who opened one eye to me, in a sort of reverse wink. I had started something, and now it was out of my hands.

That was the way it went for the next few weeks. Jake and Harry came to school every afternoon and took the Sixth Reader class out to the woodshed, where a pile of supplies accumulated. Jake and Harry had provided most of the materials, and I knew better than to ask questions.

It wasn't just the steam engine, see. We—or maybe "they", since I'd been kind of cut out, were going to plumb the library for hot water, heated, pumped up, and delivered to the librarian's tub by steam power.

I'd meant to be more involved, of course. After all, it had been me who first got interested in steam engines. But somehow the project got away from me. I could only inspect progress each day when the other children were gone. I was sorry about that, but that's the way things are, sometimes. I took comfort that Peggy was deep in, holding her own just fine with all those men-folks. She was probably the smartest of them all, and definitely best at math, though she and I both knew better than to rub it in.

Too bad none of us was quite smart enough.

About three weeks after Thanksgiving, my engineers had the Ninja Librarian and me out to the shed to look things over.

"See," Harry explained, "we've got all the stuff, and we've got the design, and we sorta wanted you to look it over and see what you think."

Their faith in me was touching, but like I say, I'd gotten pretty far behind them, what with geometry and learning to fight like a Ninja. Tom had moved me on from just breathing to a sort of slow-motion pantomime of a fight, and it was taking me all my time to learn it. So I'd not really kept up with all the ins and outs of steam engines. As for Tom, there was no saying what he did or didn't know.

I stole a glance at him, but his face was—as usual— unreadable. Certainly he studied the plans with intelligent interest. But so did I, and I was pretty sure I couldn't spot a flaw if it bit me.

"What we'll do, see," Tommy explained, "is, we'll put the engine together first, and be sure it works right. Then we can lay the pipe and hook it all up."

"What's lovely," Peggy pointed out, "is that though we'll have to fill the reservoir by hand the first time, after that the pump will fill it. The pump runs off the steam, and then some of the hot water is drained off to fill the tub at the library." She glanced at Tom to see how he took that.

Maybe he wasn't so inscrutable after all, because it was pretty easy to see that in his mind, he was already enjoying all that hot water.

Me, I wanted to ask about fuel, but decided not to. Either there'd be a lot more wood gathered, or Jake and Harry planned on liberating a bit of coal from the railroad. Either way, I wanted to be well out of it. So I kept my mouth shut and tried to locate the source of my unease. Maybe it was the coal—I was becoming a bit law-abiding in my new position as responsible schoolmaster. Schoolmistress, I suppose I should say.

For another week my Sixth Reader students spent their math and science time out in the shed, finishing their engine. Tom and I dropped in as we could, but the library was busy, and I had a room full of younger students to see to.

At the end of the week, the engine and pump stood proud, if not neat and shiny, behind the shed. A pile of coal had somehow appeared next to the brick firebox. None of the parts looked exactly new, but the connections seemed clean and tight, which I figured mattered more.

"Is it ready?"

"Gotta fill the re- reservoir," Hank said, carefully pronouncing the long word.

"Let's get all the children to help," I suggested. It was early afternoon and well above freezing. "We can make a line and pass the buckets down from the spring."

So for the next hour we sloshed pots of water into the reservoir, until Peg proclaimed it ready to go. Harry and Jake kindled a fire in the brick firebox.

Tommy ran for the librarian, figuring he should be there to witness this historic moment. He came back alone.

"Mr. Tom says he figures it'll take a half hour for the water to heat and the pump to start. He'll be here by then."

I looked at Wild Harry. "That sound right?"

He laid a hand on the exposed end of the great steel reservoir—where had I seen something like that before?—and gave it some thought. "Yup."

"Harry'n I'll stay out here and keep the fire goin'," Jake offered. "You keep the youngsters inside where it's warm."

That made sense to me, and I herded the children back in to do sums. "You too, Tommy, Peggy. Hank and Yance, too. They'll let us know when it's time to see the pump in action."

It was a long half hour, with all of us waiting for the call from out back telling us to come and see the pump working for the first time.

Finally, Tom came from the library, a book in one hand and an almost worried look on his face. Before he could open his mouth, Harry and Jake came panting around the corner.

"It's ready! Everyone—" Jake's call was cut off, as was Tom's simultaneous effort to speak, by a deafening roar from out back. Harry and Jake dove for the door as a few bricks landed in the yard. Their exclamations should have earned them a fine for language unsuited to a schoolroom, but under the circumstances I let it pass.

In a moment all was quiet outside, and then the noise began all over again in the schoolroom. We rushed out in a mass to see what had happened. I should've kept the youngsters away, of course, but I didn't.

Where the engine had stood, there was a hole in the ground. A dent, anyway. Our woodshed was nothing but splinters, and bricks and bits of metal had blown in a wide circle. My windows—I lived in the rear of the schoolhouse—had blown in.

But I counted us lucky: no one was killed, and when the reservoir had burst, it had put out the fire. A few bits of wood and coal smoldered in places, and the boys raced to stomp them out. The light snow that had fallen a few days before helped keep the fire from spreading.

We never did figure out exactly what went wrong. Tom had been coming to say he didn't think the pump would move enough water to keep itself running and fill our tubs, both, but that wouldn't make it blow up. Maybe a bad connection had given way, or the boys waited too long to open the pump valve. Maybe they needed more of an escape valve, because maybe the two giant horse troughs they'd welded together to make the boiler weren't up to the pressure. I thought of all that later.

When it happened, we all just stood there, looking at the devastation and feeling devastated.

Tom broke the silence. "Well," he said in his crispest librarian's voice, "I believe that raises more questions than it answers."

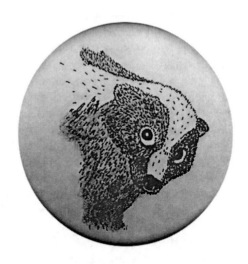

THE NINJA LIBRARIAN GETS COLD FEET

I
t was a sad and sober group of students who gathered at the Skunk Corners School a week after Thanksgiving. Behind the school, debris littered the ground for a hundred feet in every direction. The shattered remains of a dream, you might say.

Just the day before, my Sixth Reader students, with a little help from Crazy Jake and Wild Harry Colson, had fired up the steam engine they'd labored over for two months. It had taken less than half an hour to reveal a flaw in the design. Alas, we'd never know just what went wrong, because the glorious machine had blown itself—and the school's woodshed—to smithereens. Even the boiler, which I had finally identified as having started life as a pair of horse troughs, was just a couple of twisted pieces of metal on opposite ends of the yard.

I'd swept up the broken glass from my floor and covered the windows as best I could, then passed a cold night with the drafts blowing over me.

My miserable night had resolved me on one thing: I was going to get some warm coats and shoes for some of my students, come heck or high water. Winter was fixing to freeze us all, and I didn't want to lose any pupils. It also left me thinking wistfully of hot water and steam heat, especially when I had to leave my covers for the icy morning air and go light the fires, then break the ice on the water bucket to wash my face.

No point in thinking of that. I'd been cured of hankering after steam engines, and my students had been, too. I hoped.

What I needed was clothes for my students, and plenty of firewood. The latter was easy, or would be once we restacked the woodpile. We could add the splintered remains of the woodshed and I'd have plenty of fuel. That left me free to think about jackets and shoes.

My thinking had borne no fruit by the time the students arrived, but at least I had the schoolroom somewhat warm. I let the children huddle around the stove for the first while, thawing chilled hands and feet. I didn't even have to ask those with warm clothes and shoes—like Marybeth Burton, the kind though dimwitted daughter of our Mayor—to sit back and let the poorly clad ones get closer.

I studied the group while they did their morning sums. The town kids—Marybeth, Sarah, Janey, and Joey—did pretty well. They had shoes and coats, at least, however worn, and only a short walk to school. Tommy Colson always seemed to have some sort of wrap and something on his feet, usually several sizes too big and probably cast off by his brother. Wild Harry Colson could afford new shoes now and again, though it maybe didn't do to ask how.

The worst off were Billy Jenkins, Peggy Rossiter and her brother Peter, and Eunice. Hank and Yance didn't have much, but being nearly grown, they could figure it out for themselves. But the other four came farthest to school and seemed to have the least clothing. About five more walked a half mile or so and had holey shoes but some kind of wrap. They could use better stuff, but weren't in immediate danger of death by winter. Looking from those cold and ragged children to the warmly dressed town kids, I thought the less of Skunk Corners.

I hadn't gotten any bright ideas by the time we finished math and moved on to geography. All the grades studied the continents together, each child learning and sharing something. When Janey Holstead stood up with the Fourth class and reported that in Panama, it was "pretty much mostly always warm," I heard several sighs, and knew the students were thinking how nice it would be in a place that was always warm.

That did it. I'd find those kids warm clothes if it was the last thing I did. Ninja Tom would have an answer.

After lunch, Tommy and Peggy went to fetch a fresh pail of water and came back shivering. They huddled close to the stove all through the afternoon class, heads close together and whispering more than lessons would require. So I wasn't completely surprised when Tommy announced at science time that,

"Me 'n Peg need to go to the library."

"Peg and I," I corrected, adding as they went out, "No more steam engines, children." They looked at each other and shrugged. I felt convinced they still wanted to find a way to pump that spring water right down here to the school.

Seemed a good idea to me, as long as they didn't blow up anything else.

When I headed to the library after school, I had two things in mind. I'd be setting Ninja Tom to work on the problem of clothing my frozen students, and I'd warn him off any further experiments with steam engines.

"Yes, yes, of course." Tom brushed me off when I raised the question of just what Tommy and Peggy wanted.

"And Tom, we have to do something about warm coats and shoes for my pupils."

He gave me such a blank look that for the first time I thought that even a Ninja librarian might not have all the answers. I wasn't sure he'd even heard the question. I had most of the returned books shelved when at last he responded.

"I suggest you talk to Tess. I believe she might be better suited to answer such a question."

Tess Noreen was the proprietor of Two-Timin' Tess's Tavern, and while most of the ladies in town wouldn't give her the time of day, let alone ask her advice, she'd done us proud in the way of a Thanksgiving dinner at the school. I had time to see her before Wild Harry Colson—Tommy's big brother—and Crazy Jake Jenkins, who was Billy's uncle, showed up for their lessons.

Like I say, most decent women won't be seen near Tess's. I'm decent enough in my way, but somehow—maybe because I dress like a man—I get to play by a different set of rules. I walked right into the Tavern and looked around for Tess.

She was sitting in the corner with a cup of tea. It was still early, so not many men were in the place, and Johnny handled the bar alone.

"Al! Come join me in a cuppa!" Tess waved me over. She, of course, knew that whatever sort of glass I held, it was always just tea I drank. Since the place was nearly empty, I let her openly serve me in a little teacup. Then I laid out my problem.

Tess stared out the window at the chilly, muddy street. After a minute, she looked back at me.

"I have a glimmer of an idea, Al."

"What?" I wanted a solution now, but Tess just smiled.

"I'll let you know." And no more would she say, beyond, "Would you like a little more tea?"

Disgruntled, I stalked back to the library. Jake and Harry were waiting for me, so I had no time to think about my problem. Tom was lost in a pile of books, and didn't seem to notice us at all. Seemed like nobody took this to heart the way I did.

I knew better than to expect to hear from Tess in the morning before school. She worked late. Tom would be up, but he didn't come around, and I had to go through another day distracted by blue hands and feet. This time, at least I made sure my water carriers had jackets and shoes.

When I returned to my room behind the classroom at the end of the day, I was surprised to find the boards gone from the windows our little explosion had shattered. I stared at them until a voice spoke from the corner.

"Harry and Jake felt responsible. They just finished putting in the new glass a few minutes ago."

Thanks to that glass and the wintery light it let in, I could see Tess sitting before a teapot at the little table. It surprised me a bit that the keeper of the Tavern drank so much tea, but her next words drove the thought away.

"I've found the fabric for your warm coats." She nodded at a heap of green and red piled on my bed. There was something familiar about it, but I couldn't place it.

"All we need now," Tess continued, "is someone to make it up. Can the children's mothers sew?"

I thought about that. "Some."

Other children either had no mothers, or any such fabric going into their homes would end up warming someone bigger and stronger.

Tess nodded her understanding. "Then I suggest you approach the Ladies' Sewing Circle."

"Preacher Dawson doesn't like me," I protested.

"He likes me even less," Tess said. "But Miss Cornelia is the one who matters, seems to me." And Miss Cornelia was one of those who still brought food to Tom, and so fed the children. I took a deep breath and gathered the fabric into my arms.

When I passed Tess's, I knew where I'd seen that heavy velvet. The windows of the Tavern weren't bare, but they were dressed in the light summer curtains she'd removed two months back.

Tess saw me looking. "Don't worry. I've ordered replacements. No one will freeze here, either," she concluded, turning in at the door.

Miss Cornelia didn't hesitate a moment when I falteringly asked if the sewing circle could make up the coats for my students. But when, taking courage from her readiness to help, I asked about shoes, she shook her head, her smile gone.

"Shoes take money, Miss." 'Miss'? Had she been talking to Tom, determined to convert me into a girl?

"Can't someone make them?"

"No one with the know-how 'cept the cobbler. And just you catch Archibald Skinner giving anything away."

I saw her point. Well, coats were a good start.

I'd hoped to talk to Tom about shoes, but when I got to the library Jake and Harry were waiting for me, and I got no chance. Later, while Tom coached me through the slow pattern of kicks and blocks that was as far as I'd gotten in learning to fight like a Ninja, I tried to bring up the subject.

Instead of answering, Tom positioned me in a half-crouching stance and walked off upstairs.

"Hold that until I come back."

I held it until I fell over, but Tom didn't come back. When I crept up the stairs to sneak out and go home, I saw he was deep in a pile of books, oblivious to my existence. I crept past.

"Practice that stance until you can hold it forever," he said without looking up. "Every chance you get. And be sure you close the door tight when you go out. It sticks."

The next evening when I arrived at the library, there was no sign of either Tom or the boys. I'd been afraid Jake and Harry might give up studying, after the engine failed. At least they'd learned something. I looked around for what had so interested Tom last night, but found nothing. With a sigh I went and got my long knife. A little careful shaving of the door and a shot of oil in the latch, and it operated smoothly again.

Still no sign of Tom.

I went downstairs and practiced all the forms he'd taught me. When I finished, I sank into that new stance, and was still crouched there when I heard soft steps on the stairs. I tried to whirl but my muscles had frozen into place and I nearly toppled over. Tom pretended not to notice.

"Have you been practicing? Good. I apologize for my absence."

I noticed he didn't explain his absence, just apologized. I eased my cramped muscles. "I'll see you tomorrow, then," I muttered and headed for the stairs.

"Oh, Alice?" he called after me. "I shall be requiring the assistance of Messers Colson and Jenkins for a few days."

It took me a moment to sort out he was referring to Harry and Crazy Jake. I waited for further explanation, but none was offered.

"Very well. You just tell me when they want to take up their lessons again."

As I passed him on the stairs, Tom handed me a book. I pocketed it without looking at it, or him, and trudged home.

Then I slogged up the hill to the spring for a bucket of water, which I heated on the stove to something just above freezing, and took my bath.

It really was a shame our steam engine hadn't worked.

It wasn't until the noon recess the next day that I remembered the book Tom had put into my pocket the night before. I figured he'd found another story to read, or more on how to teach, to keep me from fretting while he and the boys solved the shoe problem. I pulled out the book and took a look. Not a story; it was something about woodcraft. Indian stuff, it looked like.

I flipped listlessly through the pages, hoping to distract myself from the staleness of my sandwich. I almost missed it, not paying much attention to what I was looking at, but I caught it just in time. "Make your own moccasins from just about anything," in big letters across the top of the page.

I read the whole chapter twice, mercifully forgetting all about my sandwich. When I'd finished, I sat back with a smile.

"That does answer my question, Tom," I told the empty classroom.

THE NINJA LIBRARIAN GETS THE WIND UP

I had been so excited about our new class project that I hadn't gone to the library for over a week. I hadn't so much as stuck in my head to say hello, let alone borrowed a book.

My students and I were learning to make moccasins out of pretty nearly anything, and getting something warm on their sometimes bare feet. We tried paper, bark, felt, even the occasional bit of old leather. Even the failures were fun. I had gone at it morning, noon, and night, so much that I'd even skipped my lessons with the Ninja Librarian. I had practiced the breathing, kicks, and stances he'd taught me, a little anyway. Still, I expected the sky to fall with a thump when Tom caught up with me.

So maybe I was just a little nervous when I picked the lock on the back door of the library and let myself in early Saturday morning. Once, Ninja Tom had kicked me into the dusty street for being a fool. I didn't want a repeat lesson, and I knew he didn't tolerate slacking and never heard excuses. I thought I'd come this morning and sort of ease the way, maybe pick up a book, and let him know I'd be around later for my usual fighting lesson.

But Tom didn't seem to know I'd been gone. In fact, he seemed happy to avoid any discussion of the past week, which struck me as odd. It made me nervous, like waiting for the next flash of lightning in a storm, or for a drunk to decide to start a fight in Two-Timin' Tess's Tavern.

My attack of nerves didn't last long. I hadn't known I was coming for one of my Ninja fighting lessons, but Tom had a different idea. I had barely gotten out a greeting before he had me in the middle of a brisk workout of kicks and punches. Within five minutes, I'd stopped wondering when he'd get at me for skipping lessons. He got me going so fast I scarcely had time to remove my coat.

Two hours later I stumbled back out the door, and I'd reached my own room behind the school before I realized Tom never had asked where I'd been for the last week. After a nap and a snack, my mind cleared enough to figure out there could only be one reason for it: he hadn't known.

Which meant he hadn't been there to know, and that seemed hard to swallow. Mostly it seems like Tom knows everything, no matter how I try to hide stuff, so why wouldn't he know I wasn't there—even if he wasn't either? Anyway, where would he have been besides his library?

Naturally, I had to go back, because I hadn't been able to talk to Tom at all, and I wanted to show him the moccasins the children had made—well, the ones I'd made, since most of the children were wearing theirs. That was the point, after all. Poor MaryBeth Benson, whose father is the mayor, had to wear her buttoned boots. Her mother said no daughter of hers was going to run around in "Indian shoes." MaryBeth confessed to me that her boots were warmer, but that she "felt awful out of it being the only one with no mocs."

Besides all that, I really, really wanted to know what Tom had been up to. He'd as good as told me he was up to something with Wild Horse Harry and Crazy Jake, because a week ago he'd said that they wouldn't be around for a bit. And I knew Tommy and Peggy, my top Sixth-Reader students, had been running off somewhere secret after school each day. They'd worked hard on sturdy outdoor mocs, which might be expected since they didn't have any other shoes. But there might've been extra reasons they needed them. Absorbed though I'd been in the making of more and better footwear, part of me had been listening all week for the explosion.

I brought my best cobbler's work to the library after supper Saturday. I'd made a pair of soft-topped boots out of scraps from the transformation of Two-Timin' Tess's Tavern's curtains into warm coats, and stuffed them with dried moss and leaves for warmth. Tom looked them over with interest.

"The workmanship is excellent, but the sole does seem insubstantial," he concluded.

"Good stuff for soles is awful hard to come by," I explained. "So we all made some just for indoors, to save what soles we have."

"Preacher Dawson would indubitably approve."

I stared at him in confusion. Preacher Dawson dislikes me, and the feeling is mutual. Then I caught on and laughed. Soles, souls. But I wasn't letting him distract me. "Tom, I want to know what you and those kids"—I'd forgotten that two of the "kids" were older than me—"are up to. And is it going to explode this time?"

"And is it going to provide hot water?" He asked, his eyes belying his unsmiling expression.

I felt a surge of hope, despite my worries about explosions.

Tom proceeded to crush my hopes. "To answer, in order: I'm not telling, no, and, alas, no."

I could see he was telling the truth, at least about no hot water, because he looked so sorry. For the rest, I wasn't so sure, except that he wouldn't tell me anything he didn't want to. I had no chance to learn more, because next thing I knew he had me doing drills, and he kept it up until my brain went numb.

Well, if no one would tell me what they were up to, I'd just have to find out on my own. Figuring it would be easy enough, I followed them the next afternoon.

I mean, I followed Tommy and Peggy. I knew following Tom would most likely end in me getting another kick in the seat of my pants. The kids laced up their new outdoor mocs and took off up the ridge behind the school, as though headed for the spring. I have boots, but I chose mocs too, in hopes of being quiet enough to escape notice. I slunk out the back door to trail them up the hill.

It's hard to sneak when you're Big Al. Still, I kept well back and dodged from tree to tree. The short winter afternoon helped, making deep shadows, and the kids didn't seem to notice me. They kept going past the spring, which came as no surprise, since there'd be no point in trying to hide anything there, where everyone in town came and went all day. I'd not thought the kids were just going for a drink.

Congratulating myself on my stealth, I continued following, smiling my triumph over Tom and his secrets.

Just as I was mentally patting myself on the back for being so clever, I saw something that made my heart stop. I wasn't the only one following those children.

I caught a glimpse of a tawny pelt and froze, unable to move, think, or yell. That only lasted a moment, then I heard a familiar voice call out, "Is that you, Tommy?"

I expected the lion to melt away into the forest at the sound of his voice, but it must've been young or hungry, or both, because it held its ground.

Three things happened at once.

The big cat gathered itself to leap.

Tom stepped out of the woods to meet the kids.

And I yelled.

The lion leapt right at Peggy, who didn't even have time to turn. I broke into a run, fumbling for my knife, knowing I was too far away.

Tom, moving so fast I couldn't even see him, stepped between Peggy and the lion. I tried to run faster, though I knew the beast would have completed its leap long before I could get there. Whatever happened, I'd kill the lion, I vowed.

I might've known I'd never get the chance. Tom didn't waste time with his Ninja mask, but his kick lost none of its force for all that. He met the lion with a boot-shod foot to the chest, and a blur of fist came up under its chin.

That cat reversed direction in mid-air, and flew back the way it came. Twenty feet from Tom, it hit the snow hard. Slowly, it climbed to its feet and looked at him. I knew that feeling, having been there myself.

"Don't do it, cat," I advised. It didn't. It turned and slunk off into the trees without a glance back. I felt a brief flash of sympathy for the humiliated feline.

"Let's get these kids back to the school," Tom urged, and before I knew what he was up to, we were headed back down the snow-covered path, Tommy and Peggy between us shivering from shock and fright. So I got nowhere near whatever they were working on that day. I knew Tom couldn't have arranged for that lion. I was almost sure, anyway. But he certainly did make good use of the distraction, and left me no closer to an answer than I'd been before.

I didn't manage to follow those kids the whole week after that, what with one thing and another, mostly students who wanted my help right after school and kept me busy while Tommy and Peg made their escape. To my disgust, before I found a chance to sneak after them again, Tommy and Peggy came to me.

"Teacher," Peg asked, "will you come with us? Mr. Tom doesn't want us going into the woods alone on account of that lion."

"Yeah," Tommy snickered, "he's got the wind up." Peggy elbowed him hard and he shut up, then they both went off into a fit of giggles. I eyed them skeptically. The Ninja Librarian, near as I can tell, isn't afraid of anything, except maybe widows. Certainly he's not scared of a little catamount he already kicked into the middle of next week. Just what did Tommy mean by that crack about getting the wind up?

So I slogged off up the hill after those kids, and there was no sign of the lion. He was probably three mountains away and never planning to come back. When I topped the ridge behind my students, Tom was already there, along with Crazy Jake and Wild Harry Colson. Tom looked up, and said, as though there wasn't anything unusual happening at all,

"Alice, lend us a hand with this if you will."

I looked, and there, laid out on the ground between him and the boys, was some sort of contraption about twice as long as I am tall. The thing had legs, and there was a set of holes ready dug, so I knew what was wanted when they handed me a rope. The kids grabbed it along with me, Harry and Jake hoisted from behind, and the weird rig dropped into the holes neat as Sunday boots. It stood tall on its legs, four large tin blades attached up near the top, blades that looked like they may have started life as pieces of horse troughs—or the boiler from a steam engine.

I took a good look and started to laugh. "He's 'got the wind up,' does he?" Tommy and Peggy again succumbed to giggles, while Ninja Tom and the men hooked up some connections and pretended to ignore our hoots.

In a moment, the blades of the windmill were turning. That's when I noticed that pipes led off in both directions—one set toward the spring, and the other back down the hill to the school. Water gurgled through the pipes. Tommy explained that it ran into a tub in the woods next to the school, where—I could just see it—overflow would drain off to the creek, once they'd dug a channel.

Ninja Tom stepped back, brushing dirt and snow from his trousers, and looked up at me.

"Well, Alice? Does that completely answer your question?"

First coats and shoes for the children, and now water pumped right to the school. This one answered a lot more than a question.

"Now to find a way to heat it," I heard myself say.

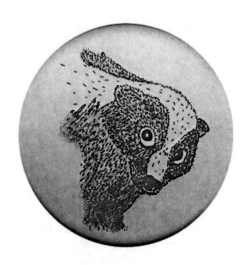

THE NINJA LIBRARIAN AND THE COURTIN' FOOL

Winter had at last begun edging on toward spring. The snow that had troubled my students so much a month or so back had become a pleasant memory, now that time—and warm sunshine—had thawed our toes and blunted our recollections. Everyone in Skunk Corners, seemed like, had taken to going for walks in the woods and along the creek.

Well, we all had our own reasons for getting out. Crazy Jake and Wild Harry Colson were busy with some grand scheme or other—finding gold or trapping chipmunks for their pelts, I suppose. It's always something with those two, and though I'd taught them to read and cipher and even to think of finding work on the railroad, I couldn't break them of chasing rainbows.

I'd long since learned that rainbows, like rabbits, always stay a jump ahead. Well, they'd settle down with the weather, and at least their new math skills would help them figure up their losses when reality hit.

Most folks went walking just to enjoy the feel of the sun on their faces, or to hunt up the wild greens sprouting all over the hills. It'd been a hard winter and we all longed for fresh things. The kids swarmed over the creek and enjoyed just messing around.

At the little one-room Skunk Corners School, I'd suspended penmanship and elocution classes in favor of nature study. I'd take the kids out to the creek after lunch to figure out the best spots for crawdads, or we'd climb the hill to follow the path of spring up the mountain. When we came back, we could all wash up and get a drink from the over-flow pipe at the windmill-fed basin by the schoolhouse.

Nights still got cold, so I mostly spent my evenings at Two-Timin' Tess's Tavern, keeping warm and drinking tea from a whiskey glass. Tess is a good friend and never lets on to anyone that Big Al doesn't drink anything stronger than coffee—or spring water in melt time, which is heady enough. Of course, I'd only go to Tess's after spending an hour or so in the library basement learning, one move at a time, to fight like a Ninja. Like the Ninja Librarian.

Even Ninja Tom must've been feeling the spring, because one afternoon when I showed up, he suggested we go for a walk and hunt up the catamount that'd tried to jump a couple of my students a while back.

"Wrassling a cat would be just the thing to test your progress, Alice." Tom is the only person who calls me by my given name. The rest of the town calls me "Big Al," and they let me get away with dressing like a man and hanging around at the Tavern. I think some folks never have figured out I'm a girl.

Tom made his joke about the wildcat, but he was serious about getting outside, so we headed down to the creek to practice. A few of the kids were about, but we found an unused sand bar downstream, where the creek levels off in the meadow and the water has time for things like sand bars.

After a while, Tom wandered off on some quest of his own, leaving me to practice the drills. I'd been doing just that, my mind contentedly empty, for I don't know how long, when my peaceful mindlessness began to be disturbed by the sense that I was not alone. Tom had told me that the discipline of my Ninja studies would make me more aware, but truth is my haphazard life before coming to Skunk Corners had done a pretty good job of it already. Of making me alert, I mean.

I kept working. I didn't want whoever watched to know I'd spotted them, so I just rotated slowly in my drills until I found the quiver in the bush that gave them away. I had figured it'd be some of my pupils, planning to jump out at me, and I was prepared to give them the lambasting they wanted. To my surprise, the next time I looked that way, I spotted a man's face. That nearly made me break my form.

I'd never seen the man before, and I didn't much like the way he was hiding and watching. I am quite able to defend my virtue, despite those who believe I don't have any. But I admit I was a bit at a loss how to deal with someone who just hid and looked. I mean, I couldn't just turn around and clobber him, could I?

I'd about made up my mind to confront the galoot when Tom reappeared and, with a crackle of brush-shaking haste, the watcher vanished. Tom turned toward the noise, but there was no one in sight.

"Some kind of varmint, I expect," he said after a moment. "Or perhaps one of the children, if so be it there's a difference."

I laughed. Tom likes the school children almost as much as I do, and is just as reluctant to admit it. I told him about the unknown watcher. Neither of us could figure who it might be.

That evening I found out. As usual, I'd repaired to Tess's for a hot meal and a drink before bed. Tonight, there was a stranger in the Tavern, a long-legged galoot whose face I knew right away. The watcher. I ignored him and went to my usual seat at the end of the bar. Tess brought me my drink and a plate of venison stew, and leaned over the bar.

"Yon tall fellow," she tipped her chin in his direction, "wanted to know who was the lovely young lady doing a strange dance down by the creek. I figured he must've meant you."

"What'd you tell him?"

"That if he had any legitimate business with any of the young women of this town he'd have spoken then and there and introduced himself properly. But I don't reckon," she added as she turned away, "that'll stop him from making a nuisance of himself."

Tess was right, as usual. If her line of work has taught her nothing else—which it has—it's taught her to read men. She'd been gone for about one shake of a coon's tail when a lot of long limbs organized themselves on the next barstool, and a kind of squeaky voice drawled,

"Kin I buy ye a drink?"

I fixed him with my best schoolmarm glare. "You appear to have taken me for someone else, mister."

"Aw, I take yeh fer the loveliest thing I ever saw."

I almost dropped my tea, but I kept my head. "Tess!" I called. "This gent has had enough. He's seein' things."

"Nothin' that ain't there, I tell yeh, miss," he leaned closer to assure me. I was so flummoxed I didn't know what to do. In all my life, no one had ever spoken to me so. This fellow had to be drunk or crazy. Or up to something. Maybe all three.

Johnny moseyed down the bar and looked the fellow over. He's Tess's barkeep and bouncer all in one, and while he's not as dangerous as our librarian, there's no denying he looks fiercer. Now he fixed my would-be swain with a cold eye and told him, "The lady says she doesn't know you. It is entirely her choice whether she wishes to know you." He turned to me. "Should I throw him out?"

The galoot turned a little pale, but to give him his due, he held his ground while I made up my mind.

"Naw, Johnny. He's just leaving anyway." Truth is, I didn't know what to think. Some tiny, undeveloped part of me thought it was kind of . . . flattering. . . to have someone talk to me so. But this fellow didn't strike me so well. It wasn't so much the "kin yeh" and the "ain't" as it was the way he smelled. Like he'd not changed his drawers all winter, but also the kind of smell you mean when you say you smell a rat. I met his look coldly, and he backed down off his stool. He was game, though.

"Wal, then, so I am. But ah'm pleased to meetcher. Name's Neb Jones."

I didn't ask about the name, but he told me anyway.

"Neb for Nebuchadnezzar. Ma figgered with a name like Jones I needed something strikin'."

Struck me, alright. Struck me like a fraud. But even while I thought that, he stuck out his hand and I shook it out of habit. Then he ambled for the door.

I looked at my hand. "Tess? Could I go have a wash?"

All week, seemed like everywhere I turned Neb Jones was there, just sort of hovering. People were noticing. Even Tom commented.

"Who's the conquest, Alice?"

"Conquest?"

"The young man who appears to have a vast appreciation of your virtues."

"He claims his name's Neb Jones. I haven't cared to find out more. I first saw him by the creek," I added to be sure Tom understood.

Tom made a thoughtful sound, which I couldn't read.

"Tom, I helped you out with those widow-ladies. Couldn't you. . . ?"

Tom drew back in a hurry. "No, Alice. That was a completely different matter. No, in this case, you are on your own."

And no matter how I argued that it was exactly the same thing, he wouldn't budge.

And I thought librarians were supposed to be helpful.

I put up with Mr. Jones for a week. Any normal fellow would have taken a hint from the way I turned down every offer of drinks, meals, and moonlit walks, and taken himself off to avoid frostbite. Apparently, Neb Jones wasn't normal, because nothing discouraged him. I finally lost patience.

"Mr. Jones, I will *not* walk out with you," I said for the fortieth or fiftieth time.

"Aw, c'mon, Alice," he began, having learned my name I don't know how. Probably guessed. But that was the last straw. No one but Tom calls me Alice, and that's the way I like it.

"I will not. I will not go anywhere with you because you are an unknown fellow with no good reason to be here, and you hail from Two-Bit, where all the low-lifes gather." Wild Harry Colson had found that out for me. "You do not have permission to use my given name, and finally, I won't go near you because you stink." We were in Tess's Tavern, and I said it all loudly enough for everyone to hear. Several people snickered. I figured that would settle him.

He left then, but I had an uneasy feeling about Neb Jones.

By then, everyone in town was speculating on the eventual outcome of this strange courtship. I had to reassure my students that no one was going to take me away from them, and it made me mad. I mean, obviously the townsfolk weren't taking my refusals any more seriously than Neb Jones himself. Did folks think I was so desperate I'd take anything?

So it was in no tranquil mood that I left Tess's after making clear my objections to the galoot from Two-Bit. I was deep in my thoughts, wondering how to get rid of the fellow so I could go back to enjoying my evenings. Tom had again refused to interfere, which annoyed me. Hadn't I helped him? Wasn't that what friends did?

I was so deep in my thoughts that an arm out of the dark was around my neck before I knew anyone was there. For one brief moment I froze as my nose told me who had grabbed me, even before he whispered,

"Now Ah hev yeh at last."

Then I discovered that Tom *had* helped me, because I was moving before my brain even registered what was needed, and the problem was being dealt with.

Now, maybe I didn't move quite as fast as Tom would have, and maybe I didn't throw him as far. But it was enough, because I tossed Neb Jones on his head, then kicked him down the street to the depot.

Someone brought a lantern from the Tavern, and when the light shone on him, he gave one "eep" and legged it out of town, back up the trail to Two-Bit.

I stood in the street, brushing the dust from my hands and feeling pretty satisfied. I heard a soft step behind me, and Tom asked, in a calm librarian's voice,

"Does that completely answer your question?"

I looked down the street where Neb Jones was just a bit of dust, and glanced back at the townsfolk who had come out to see the commotion.

"I don't know." I glared at the crowd. "Does that answer your question? Do you know now that I mean what I say?"

Tess held the lantern high and grinned as the nods and murmurs of agreement rippled through the crowd. I turned back to Tom.

"Well then, yes, Tom, I believe it does."

THE NINJA LIBRARIAN AND THE
MISLED MINERS

Skunk Corners' Ninja Librarian politely ceased rummaging through a stack of new books when I came in. I nodded and kept moving toward the basement stairs. I take my Ninja-fighting lessons in the library basement, and Tom expects me to be on time. Once I'd been ten minutes late because I had to break up a playground fight, and he'd kept me practicing so long I missed dinner at Tess's and had to eat my own cooking.

"I wondered if you could help me with something, Alice." He thumped the stack of books. "I purchased these in hopes people could learn things to make their lives easier. But we have struck on the usual shoal."

Rebecca Douglass

I guessed he meant that the people who most needed the help were unable to read. We'd had the same problem with story time, and convincing the mothers to take books to read to their children.

Tom read my thoughts, which he seemed to do often. "This time it's not just the ones who can't read who won't take them."

"They don't figure any outlander who writes books can teach them anything about the stuff they've done all their lives," I said.

"Right."

"Well," I said, and stopped. I changed the subject. "How about my lesson?" I'm one local who knows an outlander can teach me.

"What about Jake and Harry?"

All winter I'd been teaching the Three Rs to Crazy Jake and Wild Harry Colson before my Ninja lessons.

"They're still off chasing rainbows."

"I have it on good authority that they are hunting the long-lost Drunk Swede Mine," Tom told me. "I believe Harry's mother gave them twenty pounds of flour and a large sack of jerked venison and told them not to come back for at least three weeks." That sounded about right, though I wondered how he'd known, when I didn't.

An hour later I came back up the stairs more slowly than I'd gone down, and headed to Two-Timin' Tess's Tavern for some dinner. Most of the time, Tess's is a pretty quiet place, for a tavern. To my disgust, when I walked in that night, with the sun not yet down and most Skunk Corners folk still at whatever they did all day, the place was jam-packed and louder than a rainy-day recess. After a day in the classroom, I like my peace, but I like Annie's cooking even more, so I shoved my way through to the bar. A large, filthy miner occupied my stool. I thought about

114

asking him to move, but I didn't want to start something with twenty rough strangers. Especially not without my dinner.

Johnny came right over. "Evenin', Al. Tess said to send you to the kitchen," he added, low-voiced. "She says she ain't feeding this crowd."

Tess was in the kitchen, as were all the girls.

"Tess! What the dickens—?" I didn't need to finish the question.

"Miners. Prospectors. Rowdies. Word," she added grimly, "has gone out that the Drunk Swede Mine has been found."

"Have you seen Harry or Jake?" I asked cautiously.

"They haven't been around for weeks." Tess looked me over, considering. "I take it they are somehow behind this?"

I told her what Tom had said. "Do you suppose they actually found it? But where are they, then?"

Tess snorted. "Those two? They couldn't find— But they must be up to something."

No doubt. Those two were always up to something.

"Well," Tildy put in, "if they've brought this mess of low-lifes down on us, you wait 'til I get my hands on those misbegotten mistakes."

"Now, Tildy," Tess soothed, "you know the boys never mean any ill. Still," she added with a sigh, "I wish they'd stuck to selling chipmunk pelts."

I'd been shoveling in stew the whole time we talked, and now wiped out my bowl with a piece of bread. "Thanks, Annie. Good stew tonight. Tess, I take it you and the girls are staying out of there for the duration?"

Tess shrugged. "They wouldn't behave, so we left. I suppose I'll have to go back, though. Poor Johnny can't do it all."

I didn't like to think of Tess or any of the girls out there with those rough men. "I'll go. They think I'm a boy." Tess tried to protest, but I shushed her. "You know I can take care of myself."

So Johnny and I slung the booze until way past my bedtime, and no one caught on about me bein' a girl. What locals came in didn't stick around, and we closed down a mite early.

What with one thing and another, I didn't give much thought to Tom's problem. I kept busy all week helping Johnny, and all I could learn was that someone had sold someone the Drunk Swede Mine, or they were about to, or something. Half the men were hoping for jobs in the mine, and half meant to go find their own treasure, just as soon as they figured out where it was. Meanwhile, they were camped down by the creek, making a mess, and infesting the Tavern night and day.

I wanted to toss the bums out, but Tess convinced me to hold off. No one had caused any real trouble, and Tess had decided to serve dinners after all, once Johnny and I had made it clear the girls were not for grabbing, and we were making good money. Of course, there were half a dozen fights each night, but as long as they stuck to fists and didn't break the furniture, we didn't mind.

No one had seen Wild Harry Colson or Crazy Jake.

Each afternoon when I came to the library for my lessons, Tom asked if I had an answer for him, and each time I said I was still thinking. He still hadn't convinced any one to take out the books on gardening, preserving, or sewing he'd had sent in.

"After the way your students took to making moccasins last winter," he lamented, "I thought there would be more interest." Something about the comment itched in my mind, but I was trying to master a particularly difficult kick and it got away.

I arrived at Tess's in time for a quick dinner before tending bar. It was a good thing the morrow was Sunday, because I needed a long sleep. Tending bar half the night was no way to prepare for school, and my kids deserved better. I had to get these rough fellows out of Skunk Corners. They took too much keeping.

Around ten, I charged into the kitchen to change dirty glasses for clean, and found two wet, dirty, tired and frightened young men cowering in the corner by the stove. Annie had given them some food and an earful.

Jake and Harry jumped when they saw me, and I glared at them, ready to let fly with all my irritation at what they'd brought down on our town. But they looked like a pair of whipped puppies, desperate for help, and I relented. Some. Harry gasped,

"Fer Gawd's sake, don't tell anyone we're in here. They'd kill us." Jake nodded his agreement. There was no trace of the light-hearted boys who'd helped blow up a steam boiler and build a windmill over the winter. They were scared.

And they were right to be scared. The men in the other room were starting to get restless, after a week of waiting for news. I glanced back to be sure the door was shut, and hissed,

"What have you two idiots done now? All those fellows out there seem to think someone's found that Drunk Swede Mine you were after."

Harry cringed at my tone, but Jake spoke up.

"We sold the Drunk Swede Mine, and told the world."

I stared. "You sold. . . you mean you actually *found* it?"

The boys shook their heads. I sat down, feeling a bit weak in the knees. "So you sold a mine you don't own and can't locate," I said, just to be sure.

They nodded.

"And all those men. . . you'd better start at the beginning."

"Well," Harry began, "we weren't getting' nowhere huntin' the mine."

Big surprise.

"An' we ran low on grub. Ma'd said not to come back for more, so we had to do somethin'."

"We tried to sell some treasure maps we'd drawn up, but no one would buy," Jake complained.

"Then Jake got a bright idea." Harry sounded a little bitter. "We went on to a new place where no one knows us. Rode into town separate, like we never seen each other before. Jake, he let on as how he'd found the Drunk Swede Mine, but he'd gotten word his old Ma was sick and he had to have money quick to get home to her. So I made a big show of buying his map and having him sign over the mine to me, then he left and I managed to sell a few shares to get me started. Said I'd be back to hire miners, then rode out an' we took off."

"Only," Jake said, "somehow they found out we were from Skunk Corners. Those men," he nodded to the other room, "will rip us apart if they find us. They're sure to know by now it's all a fake."

"You never sold shares to all those fellows out there!"

"No, but the ones wanting work are just as disappointed. And maybe even madder if they find out there's no mine."

I figured he might be right. For a minute, thinking of the mess there was going to be, I thought about letting the mob have the idiots.

Well, whatever they'd done, I couldn't let Harry and Jake get torn to pieces in Tess's place. "First thing, let's get you out of here. The library, I think. We can get there the back way."

Jake shook his head. "We tried that. It's all locked up."

I gave him a pitying look for his ignorance. "Doesn't matter. Come on."

Once the boys were tucked away in the library basement, I went in search of Tom. Eventually, I found him in Tess's kitchen, enjoying one of Annie's hot biscuits with gravy.

"I believe it's time we did something about this crowd," was his greeting.

"What? I don't think they're going to leave just because we ask nicely."

"Perhaps not. But I think I shall begin just so."

I was right on his heels, and first thing through the door, I gave Tess the signal to get the girls out of there. Johnny'd stay. He probably had a shotgun under the bar, but I hoped he wouldn't need it. Bullets make nasty splintery holes in floors and walls, and blood is desperate hard to clean up.

Tom walked to the center of the room and began to speak. He has a special way of projecting his voice, and it took only a moment for silence to fall so everyone could hear him.

". . . is no Drunk Swede Mine, and in fact there never was. I believe you gentlemen have been pursuing an illusion."

It took them a moment to work out his meaning, just long enough for me to step up alongside. Not too close, though. My gut told me we'd need room to work.

My gut was right. When the idea sank in that they'd been hoaxed, half the miners jumped Tom as a liar trying to trick them into leaving so's he could have the gold himself. The other half attacked him as the bearer of bad news, demanding he turn over the "low-life lyin' sidewinders" who'd tricked them.

Tom couldn't have done that if he'd wanted to. He was too busy shedding enlightenment on the crowd. His kicks and strikes were so fast and beautiful that at first I just stood aside and admired. Then someone leapt on me, yelling,

"Get this Al feller! I reckon he knows somethin'."

My kicks aren't as fast or as strong as Tom's, but I did pretty well for myself. I picked up a cut over my right eye, when I got in the way of a flying bit of broken chair. Someone tried to brain Tom, and he knocked the thing aside with, as he apologetically explained later, "a trifle over-much enthusiasm." Other than that, neither of us suffered any hurt.

One by one, we pitched the brawlers out the door. Others left under their own power when they saw the way things were going. As the last of the ruffians limped out of town, watched by a lot of silent but armed townsfolk, I looked around. Johnny stepped coolly away from the kitchen door and stowed something under the bar. Not a shotgun. He'd defended the place with a baseball bat.

Tommy Colson's bat, I learned later. He'd brought it that afternoon and told Johnny to hold it for him. "Maybe right nearby where you can get at it quick," he'd suggested. Tommy's Harry's little brother, though Tommy has twice the brains and six times the sense. I guess he knew the boys were home.

Tess came out of the kitchen, demanding, "Where are those half-wits?" I didn't hesitate.

"Library basement." They didn't deserve to die at the hands of a mob, but they deserved whatever Tess did to them.

That night I dreamed about books, not battles, and next day I brought my students to the library and stood back while they made a rush for Tom's instructional books. He handed out book after book on gardening, preserving, woodcraft, and tanning hides.

"What on earth are they going to do with those?" he inquired, as the children filed out. "I don't think it will work well if they try to tell their parents how to do things."

"No. But I assigned them to learn to do something they've never done, using only the book's instructions. Then they have to prepare a lesson on it to teach the class. I suggested they try their lessons in front of other people for practice."

"And you think. . . "

I shrugged. "It's worth a stab. Does that—?"

Tom interrupted me, a dreamy look in his eyes. "Perhaps someone will learn how to make hot water. *Lots* of hot water."

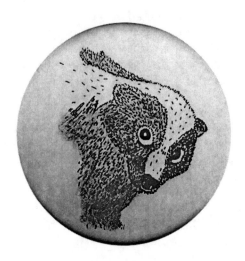

THE NINJA LIBRARIAN TAKES ON A BABY

I thought I was over being surprised by Tom, Skunk Corners' Ninja Librarian. If I'd stopped to think, I'd have known that was a silly notion.

I walked into the library one Saturday morning in May and found the Ninja Librarian standing in the middle of the room. The surprise was the tiny baby squalling in his arms.

Tom is calm and cool in the face of any crisis or unexpected development. Even when our boiler blew up and hopes of hot water evaporated, he barely quirked an eyebrow. I am trying to learn the same self-control, with limited success. That morning, sweat beaded his face.

"New patron?" I joked, glancing around for the mother. No other adult was in sight.

Tom just shook his head. He had to raise his voice to be heard over the increasingly loud noises produced by the tiny bundle in his arms. "When I got the book box this morning—" he made a vague gesture with one hand, then grabbed for the wriggling bundle again. Tom had recently taken to putting a box on the doorstep at night so folks could drop off books. And, apparently, other things.

I couldn't help it. I laughed. And all Tom could do was glare at me, for fear he'd drop the infant if he moved.

"It's sure to be some kind of joke," I gasped. "Who would leave a baby at the library?"

Tom took a firmer grip on his sense of humor—and the baby—and suggested, "Perhaps someone thought babies are like books—check one out for a few weeks then return it."

But if this was a joke, it wasn't very nice. The baby needed a mother's attention, and soon. "How old is it? Boy or a girl?" I leaned closer to investigate, and an unpleasant aroma joined the howling in assailing my senses. "Uh-oh."

Tom's look of mingled disgust, desperation, and pity set me to laughing again.

"Alice, you have to help me. I have no idea what one does for a baby."

"No more have I," I pointed out, when I could stop laughing.

"Well, but." He stopped. We both knew he'd nearly said, "But you're a woman," as though that conferred some mystical understanding of infants. Or maybe that, as a teacher, I must understand children of all ages.

This tiny waif presented a problem that neither Ninja skills nor library books could solve, but the poor thing had to be changed and fed, and soon.

Naturally, we took it to Tess.

Two-Timin' Tess's tavern wasn't open, but Tess and the girls, just finishing breakfast, gave us their full attention. It would have been hard not to, as the damp bundle Tom clutched—I'd adamantly refused to take it from him—howled louder than ever. I would never have believed such a tiny thing could make so much noise. Nor had the aroma of soiled diaper diminished.

Tom cut off any smart remarks before they started. "Someone," he announced, "left this on the library steps, apparently under the misapprehension it was a library book."

"And what do you expect me to do about it?" Tess asked coolly.

I caught a hint of a smile in her eyes, and knew Tess wouldn't let us down. Tom, by way of proving how deeply rattled he was, took her question at face value.

"Well," and for the first time I heard him sound unsure, "I'm hoping someone here knows what to do with such a creature."

Tess tried to continue her stern masquerade, but several of the girls pushed in to coo over the baby, lifting it from Tom's awkward grip—to his immense relief—and uttering strange soothing noises.

"Why, the little thing's soaking wet," Tildy exclaimed. "No wonder he's yelling."

"He?" I asked. Could she tell just by looking at that scrunched-up red face?

"Only a man-thing would yell so loud over a little discomfort," Tess claimed. I wasn't so sure, but figured we'd find out the truth soon enough. Tildy and Julia were already unwrapping the ghastly diaper, laying down a shawl on the bar to cushion and warm the infant. Julia whisked away the filthy rags that wrapped the baby, and Tildy snatched a bar towel to serve as a replacement nappy.

A moment later, Annie emerged from the kitchen bearing a beer bottle with the cut-off finger of a kid glove fastened over the top. She shook a little of the contents out onto her wrist, then cuddled the freshly-swaddled boy—as it had, in fact, turned out to be—into the crook of her left arm and held the bottle to his mouth with her free hand. The squalling ceased at once, replaced by quiet slurping noises. I was close enough to smell the warm milk, so I didn't worry about the beer bottle.

Tom seemed to figure he'd found the solution to his problem, and began edging toward the door. Tess grabbed his arm.

"Where do you think you're going? You'd better start learning how to take care of this baby."

Tom gestured vaguely. "Can't you all keep it—him—here? The girls seem to like him, and they know what to do."

Tess shook her head, and this time there was no hidden laughter. "We can't. You know the sort of talk that'd make, and the assumptions folks'd make about the place."

I was a little surprised, because I'd always figured—well, never mind.

"So how did you all get to know so much about babies?" I blurted, then turned red as a hatless greenhorn.

"Well," Annie said, "I lived with an aunt who had a new baby every year, like clockwork. Soon's I could, I got away, but it wasn't so soon but what I learned I'd rather cook than tend babies all day."

Tildy nodded. "Oh, honey, you don't get to my age without learning a thing or two." I had no idea how old Tildy was, but I didn't think that was much of an answer.

Julia laughed. "Maybe so, Tildy, but I learned most of what I know about children long before I was Al's age, only it was my own Ma taught me. I was the oldest of fifteen. I think."

No wonder she'd come here. A tavern in Skunk Corners had to look pretty good next to that. I was beginning to think there was something strange about my own raising.

"Don't you have any brothers or sisters?" Hilda asked.

I shook my head. "No, nor any Ma, either. Just me and Pa, till he died." That'd been when I was fourteen. I'd managed a couple more years in Endoline before finding my way to Skunk Corners— and a school full of kids. But by the time I get 'em, they can take care of themselves, mostly.

I felt Tom's eyes on me, almost as pleading as the babe's, but I shook my head.

"I can't afford the gossip either, Tom, even if I knew what to do for him."

Annie was holding the baby out to Tom, and he automatically reached for it. She helped him settle the now-sleeping infant more comfortably.

"Well, perhaps my reputation can stand the gossip," Tom said dryly, "but I fail to see how I can manage by myself. It scarcely seems the sort of thing books help with, nor did my training cover the care and feeding of infants."

"Oh, I don't know," Tess murmured. "I'm sure there are books that teach about babies, just like gardening and tanning hides."

"And it would just be until we can find his mother," I put in. Tess and Tildy exchanged glances, and it occurred to me that the mother might not want to be found. Even so, I didn't think Tom would be left on his own for long. Once the word got out, some of the townswomen would be willing to care for the baby.

I took a great deal of delight in Tom's discomfiture, all the same.

I was able to go on taking delight for the next several days. Tom's rooms became a chaos of bottles, blankets, and nappies, and the place began to develop an aroma that told me that someone was going to have to step in and do some washing, at least.

The library would have stayed closed, except I came in every day after school and opened it. The first day, Tom didn't even leave his room, but after that, he brought the baby out whenever possible, in hopes that someone would claim it, or at least recognize it.

No one did.

Along about Wednesday I snuck out while Tom was holding court, gathered up all the filthy clothes and dirty nappies, and bundled the lot over to Tess's. I left the reeking bundle out back and went in to see if there was hot water—and maybe some help doing the washing. Besides, I wanted to talk to Tess.

She spotted me right off. "Hey, Al. How are things at the library?" She didn't try very hard to hide her smile.

Nor did I. "Oh, Tom's a wreck, and I haven't had a lesson since the baby came, but lots of folks are coming in. No one's recognized the little squawker, though."

"I didn't suppose they would. Did you bring the washing?"

Now, how did she know that? I was beginning to think Tess had studied the same place Ninja Tom had, the way they both seemed to read my mind.

"Yes." I changed the subject. "I sort of expected someone would offer to take the child by now."

Tess was shaking her head, and grinning widely. "A couple of the ladies were all in a rush to take the poor mite home and care for it," she began.

"So why didn't they?" I interrupted.

"I stopped them."

That floored me. I mean, whose side was Tess on, anyway?

"Oh," she said, seeing my face, "only for a time. I just suggested that they wait a bit to be sure. I think the two best possibilities have been over at the library a great deal. I'm sure one will make an offer very soon. Meanwhile, it doesn't hurt Tom to learn he doesn't know everything."

When I left, I felt better, between Tess's assurances, her secret glee at Tom's discomfiture, and the meal Annie gave me. That, and the promise that the laundry would be done. I went home and spent the rest of the afternoon marking papers.

Tess' plan didn't work out quite as she'd intended. For one thing, as we should have expected, after a few days Tom got the hang of baby care—and became truly fond of the little squaller. Given how smart he is, we really shouldn't have been surprised by that.

Then the question of Baby's permanent home got more complicated.

By the time I got to the library Saturday morning, half a dozen women had arrived, and were taking turns holding the baby, cooing over his gurgles and tickling his toes and generally being absurd. Tom sat behind his desk, watching.

I assessed the crowd. Mrs. Benson, the mayor's wife, looked like she smelled a bad smell, and passed the baby off quickly to someone else. On the other hand, Mrs. Herberts, the widowed owner of the tea shop, held him as long as she could, until another woman reached eager hands for him. I recognized that one as Mrs. Holstead, the mother of my pupil Janey.

Other women of all ages took their turns with a more disinterested pleasure, happy to cuddle the baby and equally happy to pass him off when asked.

Tom sat at his desk, and studied them. I knew he was weighing each woman's claim to mother our boy. Somehow, while I was noting all this, the baby ended up in my arms. Mrs. Herberts, refusing my efforts to hand him over at once, adjusted my hold and suddenly it felt—nice. I was starting to smile when the door slammed open and a scruffy man swaggered across the threshold.

"'At 'ere's my kid and I've come ter git it."

I tried to shift to a defensive stance, but the baby in my arms prevented me. Before I could panic, Tom stepped forward, and the women closed around the baby and me.

"Exactly what do you mean, sir? You do not appear to me to be the child's mother." I heard a few snickers, quickly stifled.

"My no-good girl ran off to hev him, so I reckon he's mine."

I recognized the man. He came from Endoline, and was called Basher. He spotted me, too.

"You, Al, you know my Elly. Allus runnin' away, she is."

"Ella ran off because this lout beat her." She'd go back because she didn't know any other life. I met his gaze. "What'd you do? Kill her outright at last?"

"She done run off to hev her bebby."

Seemed Ella'd gotten with child, he didn't know by whom. Just about anyone could have taken advantage of a girl as beaten-down as Ella, I figured. In the single act of courage in her miserable life, she'd run off to protect the baby when Basher beat her. He had no idea what had become of her, or how the baby had gotten to the library, but he'd heard we had one and figured it was hers. "And Elly's my girl, so that bebby's mine."

God only knew what he would do with an infant. None of us wanted to find out.

Just when we were all bracing to fight for the child, an old woman, gnarled as a valley oak, appeared in the doorway, leaning on a crooked stick.

"Git out of here, Cecil Bashion," she ordered. We all stared blankly, until I saw Basher turning red. Cecil?

The tiny woman advanced on the big man.

"You beat Elly and starved her, but she lived long enough to hev her baby."

Basher took a step toward the woman, but Tom intervened. "I think you had best depart."

Basher growled as he turned. He raised his fist for his trademark bash. Tom did—something—and Basher lay on the floor. He got up, not too slowly, and charged at me. Again, Tom sent him flying without seeming to move. This time, Basher went clear on out the door and into the muddy street. Tom brushed some imaginary dust off his hands.

"Well, now, Ma'am, you say the child's mother is dead?"

"Buried her meeself, and brung the baby here."

"And the father is unknown?" A nod. "The grandfather is clearly unfit. Any other relatives? Ella's mother?"

"Daid. Don't reckon any un' else'd admit bein' kin to that scum."

"A valid point," said Tom. "Did Ella name the child?"

"Nope. Never said nothin' but 'take him to the Skunk Corners library.' Then she up and died, so I done it."

"Then," Tom concluded, "I believe it's time we found this boy a name and a home. I think he deserves better than Bashion."

All eyes turned to me, as I still held the baby. Then the women looked at each other, and a few began stepping back, Mrs. Burton among the first. She knew she wasn't there to adopt a baby.

In the end, there were only two women left, Mrs. Herberts and Mrs. Holstead. They looked at each other, and each had sorrow and longing in her eyes. After a moment, Mrs. Herberts' eyes filled with tears.

"I can't. I can't take care of him properly, alone as I am. You'll raise him well, Jane Holstead, and he'll help fill that hole your boy's death left."

Mrs. Holstead, who'd lost a baby the past winter, slowly reached for the child, and, with one last look at Mrs. Herberts, I handed him over.

"Let's name him James Thomas," Mrs. Holstead said. "And you, Rose, will be his Godmother." Both women were crying as they went out together with the baby.

Folks were starting to sniff and in another minute there were going to be tears and sentiment all over the place. Nodding briskly, Tom turned to the old woman standing just inside the door. "Ma'am? Does that completely answer your question?"

She looked from the two women moving down the street to the distant speck that was the departing Basher, and grinned, exposing three teeth.

"Yup."

THE NINJA LIBRARIAN AND THE
OUT-OF-TOWN TOUGHS

With the library running without a hitch, the children studying as they ought, baby James Thomas safe in a good home, Jake and Harry at work again on their studies, and everyone in town clear on the position of our Ninja Librarian, all should have been tranquil in Skunk Corners.

My students were the first to tell me it wasn't.

"Big Al! Big Al!" Tommy Colson ran in, hollering and excited. "Al, there's some toughs down at Tess's talking awful trouble. I heard when I was goin' by."

Two-Timin' Tess's was the tavern, and everyone knew such places were made for drinking too much and talking trouble, so I didn't exactly panic.

"Oh?"

"Al, no one here knows 'em. They must've come down from Two-Bit or Pine Knot, or even Endoline."

"Someone here would know any toughs from Two-Bit. Maybe even Pine Knot," I mused. Including Tommy's brother, Wild Harry Colson.

"Well, they ain't from around here, no how."

"Aren't, anyhow," I corrected, grabbing a chance to teach my students better grammar. I wasn't too concerned about toughs, local or otherwise. Skunk Corners is a pretty tough place itself, even without our Ninja Librarian.

Still, that evening when I'd finished with my Ninja lesson, and set Jake and Harry to working out some math problems, I asked Ninja Tom what he thought about it. To my surprise, he looked thoughtful.

"I have been hearing a lot of rumors about those men, though I don't know anything for certain. Did you ask Jake and Harry?"

"They haven't gone near Tess's since she pinned their ears back over that business about the Drunk Swede Mine."

Tom gave a reminiscent laugh. "I believe you." He didn't offer to visit Tess and find out what was up, either. He had definitely come off second-best over the baby, at least for a time. But the child was thriving, and had been named in part for Tom, so I didn't think he needed to feel bad.

So I headed on down to Tess's, which is what I would have done in any case, since Annie was still cooking the best meal in town. But I was just a little more prepared than usual for whatever might happen.

I'd have liked to slide in unnoticed, but I'm hard to overlook. Still, I went in quiet-like and took my usual stool at the end of the bar without creating any great stir. Johnny moved down the bar to serve me, keeping an eye on the table in the middle of the room.

I cut my eyes that way without turning my head, and knew these were the guys who had folks worried. Dusty, unshaven, and scowling, they sat in front of a litter of glasses, empty and full. If they were from Endoline, they were new since my time there.

"What'll it be, Al?" Johnny was asking.

"Dinner, and the usual." I didn't need to elaborate. Johnny keeps a bottle of tea for me, and most folks figure I'm drinking whiskey. Whiskey fits my tough image, but it makes me dizzy. Tom says my little deception is perversity. I had to agree, once I'd looked the word up.

That was neither here nor there as I sat nursing my drink and waiting for whatever Annie cared to serve me. I kept my mouth shut and my ears open. A few locals drank well away from the gang in the middle, and if they spoke, it was in low voices no one else could hear.

Not so the toughs. They weren't hollering, but neither were they being secretive. Even so, I could only catch snatches of their talk, words and phrases, aside from an occasional bawdy tale told especially loudly in order, I was sure, to embarrass the Skunk Corners drinkers, who keep things clean in front of Tess and the girls.

". . . wipe 'em up. . . good base. . . sissy town. . . even has a library!" That last caught my attention. What did they want from our library?

Maybe nothing, it appeared as I listened more intently. "A library, haw haw." A loud guffaw seemed to suggest they felt a library was a sign of degeneracy, and a sure indication we were too soft to fight.

At least one man had some doubts. I caught a few words in a less brash tone. ". . . story. . . librarian. . .

toughs. . ." Others sniggered over what they took to be an absurd tale. One voice came through clearly: "I've seen that there librarian. That there story is plain lies. He's just a fussy old feller."

I kept listening while eating the meal Tess delivered herself, but heard nothing new. After a while, I nodded to Johnny and slid from my stool. As I let the door swing shut behind me, I heard the same voice exclaim, "That there was a *girl*! Any town lets girls in their tavern runs a bit short on men, wouldn't you say?"

I nearly turned back to teach them a lesson, but common sense intervened. There were six of them, and they were armed. Big Al is tough, but not that tough. Not yet, anyway.

I felt pretty low as I stumped back to the library, and I guess I looked a bit less than cheerful, because folks seemed in a hurry to stay out of my way. It gave me a queer feeling to see them dodge, as if I were like those fellows drinking and talking at Tess's. I wasn't wearing a gun, the way the toughs were, but folks still got out of my way.

That was when I got mad, when I was telling it all to Tom. It wasn't that the fellows laughed at our Ninja Librarian, or called me a girl—"which you are," Tom pointed out—it was because if our Skunk Corners folk were scared of *me*, they'd never stop those low-down types doing whatever it was they had in mind.

"They'll just come beggin' for you to take care of it for them," I ranted. "Folks here have gotten *soft*."

Tom sighed. "I fear you are correct." He gestured out the window, and I could see the mayor, the preacher, and Doc Thorpe approaching through the dusk. I would've left, but Tom stopped me.

"Just sit down and pay attention, Alice." Not only is Tom the only one who calls me by my real name, he's the only one in town who can order me around. I sat as instructed and listed while the pillars of our community begged the Ninja Librarian to protect them from the unknown bad guys who wanted to take over their town. The town, I might add, that had tried so hard to drive Tom away when he first arrived. Not that these three had done much. Seemed to me that was just the problem.

When they finished, Tom told them that the library was his job, and the town was theirs. "I will do my job, and keep the library running smoothly. I expect you to do yours."

The town pillars stared at him, no more astonished than I was. Was I hearing correctly? The Ninja Librarian was refusing to fight for his town?

But, I reminded myself, it really wasn't his town, was it? Not only had he not exactly been welcomed when he'd first come, but he'd had to fight for every change and improvement. Who could blame him if he'd gotten tired of babysitting a town full of uneducated rowdies?

Doc stood up. He's definitely the best of the lot. "Come on, you fellows. Let's go and start planning." He turned to where I sat, thinking myself unnoticed, and put me square in the middle. "Well, Al? Are you with us or agin us?"

I looked frantically from Doc to the Mayor, who looked as flummoxed as I felt, to Preacher Dawson, who looked as though he smelled a bad smell, and finally to Tom. He just sat there with a little smile, as if enjoying my perplexity. Then I was on my feet, following the others out. I didn't look back, but Tom called after me, "I'll see you at your lesson tomorrow, Al."

Since Tess's tavern appeared to be headquarters for the unknowns, we went on past. I thought about suggesting we use the school, but Tess had come out

of the Tavern and joined us, and she had a look about
her that kept me from speaking up. A look that
reminded me that she wasn't one to be pushed
around.

Well, wasn't that what we needed? I remembered
that we'd faced other problems together and solved
them with our own wits. Hadn't we clothed the
school children? Tom hadn't done that. Suddenly, I
knew what needed doing, and knew that we could do
it.

I didn't look at the Mayor. "Mr. Burton, pass the
word. Anyone who wants to help can come down to
the church."

"The church?" Preacher Dawson squeaked. "You
would use the House of God for a war council?"

"Wouldn't be the first time, I reckon. Go on,
Mayor." That was Doc Thorpe.

I watched out the corner of my eye as Mr. Burton
carried out Doc's orders.

Tess turned on the preacher. "You don't have to
come, Preacher Dawson. But don't you get in our
way, either. I want my tavern back, and I want no
trouble in my town. If you're scared, get out."

To my surprise, the preacher squared his shoulder
and stepped up next to us. "I'm meant to be a
pacifist, Miss Noreen. But there are limits. May the
Good Lord forgive me, there are limits."

I wasn't sure what limits had been passed just yet.
Those men had done nothing but talk so far, though I
was pretty sure it wouldn't stop there. But the
Preacher had been raised right here in Skunk Corners,
so I guess the pacifist veneer wasn't any too thick.

Doc didn't say anything.

The meeting was grim. Johnny wouldn't leave the
bar, but Tildy reported that there were now ten
toughs setting there, armed and getting mean with

drink. She and the other girls, no cringing lilies, had had to leave, because the men wouldn't leave them alone. "Worse than the miners," she said. "They aren't even trying to hide their plan. They figure to take our town, on account of the depot. Then they can rob every train that comes through."

"That's stupid," I said. "The railroad people'd catch on right away and come after them."

"I suppose," ventured Preacher Dawson, "that's when these ruffians would disappear and leave us to explain."

It made sense, but no one seemed to know what to do. We couldn't fight so many armed men. Skunk Corners had its own rough element, but few went armed, and the roughest sorts had mostly left after Tom came and started civilizing us. Even Tom, Ninja or no, might've had some trouble. Remembering his refusal to help, I put him out of my mind. But if he couldn't outfight ten guns, neither could I, Ninja lessons or no.

I stopped listening to the wilder and wilder schemes being suggested by the townsfolk, and set to thinking. A long time later, I stood up. I had to shout to make myself heard.

"Siddown and shut up!" My yell, perfected in the schoolroom, penetrated the babble without trouble. "Here's what we'll do."

"You have an idea, Big Al?" someone shouted.

"No. I have our plan." That shut them up.

Really, it was simple, once I stopped thinking about force and started thinking about. . . thinking.

Tildy went back to the bar to coach Johnny on his part. The tricky bit was getting the toughs past the belligerent stage of drunk without a war breaking out, but Johnny was very good at his job. A little extra whiskey in each glass. . . and maybe a little something else, too. I'm not suggesting Johnny would put anything in a drink as a general rule, but this was no ordinary occasion.

By the time I brought the girls back from the kitchen, where they'd been nursing a grudge along with the bruises the louts had given them, the men couldn't see straight. The girls didn't even need to get flirty. They just waltzed in and told the men they had a place out back where they could spend the night. Nine of them followed Julia and Hilda out without a word. The tenth put his head down on the table and commenced snoring.

Johnny and I lugged that one off between us.

Out back on a spur track was an old bunk car, left by the railroad crew years ago when they stopped maintaining our tracks. The toughs, no longer bellicose, flopped onto the bunks. One or two made half-hearted plays for the girls, but no one seemed to care when we all left. A chorus of snores followed us out.

Most of the men of Skunk Corners, and a fair portion of the women, had come into Tess's while we were out back.

"Well, Al?" Tess demanded. "What now?"

"Now? Drinks all around, if people want them. Then we've one last little bit of work."

Half an hour later, I headed around back with a dozen of Skunk Corners' strongest citizens. A quick peek showed the toughs snoring fit to shake loose the spiders from their webs.

"All together, then. Get behind and push." I knocked the blocks from the wheels before going to join the others. I had a fleeting fear that the rail car might be too rusted to move, but Mrs. Johnson, who ran the Mercantile with her husband, had snuck back earlier with an oil can, and her efforts paid off.

We got it into place just before the westbound train pulled in. That was another tricky moment, but Hilda and Tildy sashayed up to the brakeman and engineer, armed with boxes of cookies the ladies of Skunk Corners had provided. The dual distraction worked perfectly. No one noticed when we pushed that car into place and coupled it on behind the caboose. With a toot of the whistle, the train pulled out, taking our troubles with it.

"Where do you think those fellows will end up?" Tess asked.

I shrugged. "Somewhere else. Maybe they'll go all the way to the city."

"I don't suppose they'll do much harm there. I hear they've so many like them in the city, they mostly wear themselves out fighting each other."

I didn't go see Tom until after school the next day. By then, I'd gotten my back thumped by so many congratulatory fists that I'd forgotten I was angry with him for not helping us.

"I never would have thought the people of Skunk Corners could work together so well and do so much," I admitted when I'd finished telling him about it. I fixed him with my best teacher glare. "Does that completely answer your question?"

He gave a little smile when he answered. "More importantly, Alice, I believe it answers yours."

It did. I just wasn't sure I liked the answers.

EPILOGUE

Two days later, I knew I'd been right. The Ninja Librarian had shown us we could manage on our own.

Now we had to.

ABOUT THE AUTHOR

Rebecca Douglass mostly resides in Daly City, California, with her husband and two teenaged sons. Her imagination resides where it pleases, in and out of this world. After a decade of working at the library, she is still learning the secrets of the Ninja Librarian.